A NOTE ON THE TRANSLATORS

MAUREEN FREELY is a novelist and journalist who contributes to the *Guardian* and the *Independent*. She translated Orhan Pamuk's recent novels from Turkish into English. She grew up in Turkey and now lives in England.

JOHN ANGLISS won the inaugural British Council's Young Translators' Prize for prose in 2012. He lives in Ankara.

SHADOWLESS

Hasan Ali Toptaş

Translated from the Turkish by
Maureen Freely and John Angliss

BLOOMSBURY PUBLISHING
LONDON · OXFORD · NEW YORK · NEW DELHI · SYDNEY

BLOOMSBURY PUBLISHING
Bloomsbury Publishing Plc
50 Bedford Square, London, WC1B 3DP, UK

www.bloomsbury.com

BLOOMSBURY, BLOOMSBURY PUBLISHING and the Diana logo are trademarks
of Bloomsbury Publishing Plc

First published in 1995 in Turkey as *Golgesizler* by Can Yayinlari, Istanbul
First published in Great Britain 2017
This paperback edition first published in 2018

This book has been published with the support of the Ministry of Culture and Tourism of
Turkey in the framework of the TEDA project.

Every reasonable effort has been made to trace copyright holders of material reproduced
in this book, but if any have been inadvertently overlooked the publishers would be glad
to hear from them.

This is a work of fiction. Names and characters are the product of the author's imagination
and any resemblance to actual persons, living or dead, is entirely coincidental.

British Library Cataloguing-in-Publication Data
A catalogue record for this book is available from the British Library.

ISBN: HB: 978-1-4088-5082-4
PB: 978-1-4088-5089-3
EPUB: 978-1-4088-5084-8

2 4 6 8 10 9 7 5 3 1

Typeset by Integra Software Services Pvt. Ltd.
Printed and bound in Great Britain by CPI Group (UK) Ltd, Croydon CR0 4YY

To find out more about our authors and books visit www.bloomsbury.com.
Here you will find extracts, author interviews, details of forthcoming
events and the option to sign up for our newsletters.

I

The barber raised his scissors high in the air, as if to toast my health. 'Do come in, sir,' he said.

His apprentice might have said the same thing, but his voice could not be heard; he just opened his mouth and closed it. He was circling the chair with little clipped steps, his eyes never leaving the barber. Whatever tune it was that he heard in his master's clicking scissors, he seemed to be dancing to it. From time to time he glanced over at the men sitting in the corner. These were the spectators, no doubt: they were lost in the scene, and they said not a word as the scissors kept clicking.

The clicking stopped. The customer staggered from the chair. The play had consumed him. He could barely find the strength to put on his coat. As he tipped the apprentice, he turned to the barber. 'I'm still aching inside,' he said. 'I'm still not over it . . .'

The barber said nothing; for a long time he just stood there, watching the man leave. He turned back to his customers. One shifted in his seat, as if to say that he was the next in line. The prayer beads swinging from his hand were as black as dungeons. But if this was a sign, the barber took no notice, or perhaps this was his way of letting it be known that no one danced in this establishment without his say-so. For now he turned to the man next to me, the one with the goatee. 'You're next,' he said.

'And so,' I said to myself, 'the next dance begins.' The man stood up without a word and moved towards the chair. The apprentice stood ready with the towel. The barber stood over the counter, inspecting his razors, but now and again he glanced up at the mirror to size up the man with the goatee. His eyes glinted: something in them called to mind an executioner's blade.

'Which tells me this dance will be bloody,' I said to myself. The prayer beads began to click, and there was fury in the way those little black dungeons hit against each other: their owner was a man who did not like being overlooked. The beads, not the scissors, were keeping the beat now, and they spoke of blood. All the dancers were at last in place. The man with the goatee sat waiting in the chair, bowed in silence, ready to be sacrificed. The barber had chosen his razor. The apprentice draped a white sheet around the man's shoulders and pulled it down around his knees – to catch the blood, perhaps?

A great silence descended.

Until the barber said, 'Why aren't you talking, sir?'

'What is there to say?' I said. My voice was tense, for now I, too, had been pulled into this dance.

'Say anything,' the barber said. 'All you need to do is talk.'

His opening sally, no doubt. An executioner would want to extract as much as he could from a man before summoning him to the chair. His beady eyes kept lighting up, and going dark again, the better to hide his blade.

'Are you still writing novels, for example? Talk about that.'

'I am still writing novels,' I said, in as dry a voice as I could muster. I looked up to examine the sketch he'd pinned to the wall: a giant dove, executed in charcoal. Cigarette smoke had yellowed it somewhat, and its edges were beginning to curl.

'What's it called?'

Our eyes met in the mirror.

'If you mean my novel,' I said, my voice sounding so distant, 'I don't yet know.'

The dungeon beads stopped clicking. The barber set down his brush. He gazed out into the street. The blades flashed in his little eyes again, but he was already somewhere else. He was flying through the avenues of the city, to a place far away on the other side of the mountains. Perhaps he'd left something of himself behind in that place: something that he couldn't take with him. Perhaps there was a village somewhere out there with a barber's shop just like this one, and a man dressed like a barber who turned his head now and again, to look this way.

2

Then he turned his eyes to the muhtar, who was crossing the village square. The two men waved at each other, as if from a great distance.

'You're one of us now,' muttered the muhtar, continuing on his way. He allowed himself a smile. It carried him right home, this smile, lightening his spirit and helping him forget how much the election had depleted his reserves. His wife was sprinkling olives on a lettuce salad as he passed through the gate to his courtyard.

She kept her arm raised as she asked, 'Did you win?'

The muhtar raised his hat and tossed it towards the door. 'I won,' he said. 'Once again, I'm the muhtar!'

He bounded up the stairs to the roof, settling himself cross-legged before the chimney stack. On the tray before him was a stewed chicken, its legs upraised, a saltcellar, a few sheets of yufka cut into quarters and a bottle of rakı. This was his victory feast; he had it prepared for him once every four years. Each time he took a bite, he narrowed his gaze, first looking out at the cliffs and the dark earthen rooftops of the village in their shadow, and then wetting his moustache with rakı. His moustache had yet to assume the authority that was its due; with every year, there was more white in it.

It occurred to the muhtar that there was no village further from the State than this one, and no village further from God. Each time he lifted his glass, he peered into the night and the cliffs buried inside it, longing to see all that they hid from him: the mountain peaks, the far side of that forest, those plateaux and pastures. Then he'd turn to look out at the horizon, at the plains beyond reach. What would it take, he wondered, for God to notice them, for the State to turn its head just once, and register their existence? The very notion made the muhtar want to laugh. He might as well ask himself what it would take to knock down these mountains. But that was blasphemy! He repented at once, mumbling the names of everyone from the trader to the smith, from the wrestler to the doctor. There was, perhaps, no need for him to drink this much; the State did not wait for invitations. Today or tomorrow, it could sweep in to wrest away these plains. It would raise a flag outside the muhtar's office, proclaiming its existence. This sudden miracle would surprise the old-timers, no doubt: from childhood they had been hearing about those irrigation canals that had been promised them; for a lifetime, they had been spreading this news. They had even, on the eve of an election, claimed that some men from the National Assembly had come to the plain to argue about which way the canals should go – that they'd used their ropes and spades and measured out the routes. Though in fact, no one from the village had seen anyone out there on the plain. They couldn't have done; by the time they'd walked down the dozens of roads to reach these men, they'd have been halfway back to the capital.

The muhtar downed what was left in his glass. He stroked his moustache. He was cold; and yet again almost out of breath. He did up his jacket and for a time he tried to shrink himself inside it, until a button came undone and he had to straighten himself out.

Then he found himself with his wife, in his son's arms, at the top of the stairs. His wife was saying nothing, but his son was shaking his head and muttering under his breath. What he said made no sense to the muhtar, who kept turning around to stare into his son's face. Even this was beyond him when they began the descent; whenever his head lolled forward, he could hardly breathe. He was approaching his bed when, with a great roar, he began to vomit. Tomato slices came surging up. Ragged lettuce leaves hung from his mouth. His eyes bulged like a bull's; with one hand he cradled his stomach, while with the other he grasped at thin air. His head hit the pillow, and he took a deep breath. How long had he been up there on the roof, drinking rakı? All night long, probably.

'Today you are not to wake me until evening,' he said.

3

The barber was still at his window, watching the village square. His eyes glinted like executioners' blades.

Since arriving in this place, he had not said a word, apart from the few that were absolutely necessary. Had he wished to speak, he'd not have known what to say, for he could recall nothing of his past. He knew only that he'd travelled a great distance, a very great distance. But he had no memory of the place he had left, and neither did he know if it had been his intention to come to this village, or what roads he had travelled, with what purpose. In his mind he had dreamed up a hundred possible answers, and killed each one off. 'Maybe I lived in a city,' he had said to himself one day. 'In a house with a balcony, for instance, overlooking a garden. With a wife, the sort you might see in a dream. And children. And a shop, of course, if I'm a barber. On a busy street, on the corner. And customers: some young, some old, some who wouldn't stop talking, others who wouldn't say a word . . . I had my problems. And also, my customers' problems. There were things I couldn't buy, things I couldn't sell, things I couldn't do or say, and places I couldn't go . . .'

Had he had enough of all that? Had he prised himself from the city's grasp and fled to the mountains? Had the barber thrown the tools of his trade into a suitcase and set out into the darkness, to wander lost through the enchanted night? What mountains had he crossed, and what plains? Had he somehow known that Cıngıl Nuri, the village's only barber, had chosen that moment to abandon his profession, and come down from the mountains to plant himself in front of the muhtar's office?

Not one of these questions could he answer.

For all he knew, he could still be living in a city. He could be in his shop at this very moment, with his back to the soaps and creams, looking through the window, watching the street. Unless his eyes had already taken him off to the back of beyond, to a place so far away that even the customer with the goatee had never seen it.

4

When the muhtar opened his eyes the next morning, he found his wife leaning over him. 'Get up,' she said. 'Get up. Reşit wants to see you.'

It felt like a dream; a brown cat with a long tail was circling his wife's feet. Its eyes were two wells of fire.

'Tell him to wait,' said the muhtar, 'I'm on my way.'

He looked again at the cat's eyes. He had seen these eyes before, burning like embers, down to the last detail. But when? He sat up, clutching his forehead. No answer came to him. His wife and the cat headed for the door, while he sat there, watching them go. For a long time, he just sat there, rubbing his moustache, as if to rid it of his aniseed breath.

Then suddenly it came to him. He remembered when he had seen a cat's eyes burn like embers. The day after he had first been elected muhtar, sixteen years ago, he had again opened his eyes to see his wife.

He couldn't even have said it was his wife, in fact, for he'd seen nothing more than a slow fading shadow, leaning over the bed and saying, 'Get up.' In exactly the same way as his wife had done, only a moment ago. 'Get up. Cıngıl Nuri's wife wants to see you.'

That day, the muhtar hadn't told her to wait; eager to take on his first duty, he'd jumped out of bed and into his clothes. Bounding through the door, he had gone straight across the yard to take Cıngıl Nuri's wife by the hands. The three children she had brought with her had looked up at him in fear. At first, the muhtar had been surprised; he hadn't known where to put his hands or where to leave them. Then, thinking that a muhtar should be the last person in a village to be taken by surprise, he hid himself inside a cloud of cigarette smoke and gave the children a smile.

The woman's eyes were two fountains, her hair flew wild and she had beaten her knees until they were sighing with pain. She told him that her husband had left the house saying that he needed room to breathe, lest his soul vanish from the face of the earth. He had never come back. As their mother spoke, the children had lined themselves up next to her, like a string of prayer beads. 'They're looking for the head bead,' the muhtar had said.

Then the woman had described what her husband had eaten the previous day, what he had talked about, how he had looked at the birds in the sky when he was walking home from his shop, why he had slapped his little girl on his way into the house, and what shirt he had been wearing when he'd sighed and said he needed room to breathe; then she'd asked where he could have gone, if he could have been murdered and thrown into a creek, if he was now food for the vultures, or if he had fallen from the cliffs, or gone to visit the forty saints.

The muhtar had listened to her calmly, gauging her every word as confidently as if he'd been muhtar for a thousand years. All this while, he'd kept himself safe inside the clouds of smoke rising from the cigarettes he was chain-smoking. Refusing to believe that a man could be lost to anything but the grave, one villager had insisted that it was just not possible: a man could not just vanish. Without a doubt, Cıngıl Nuri had gone off somewhere; probably, he was on a bender. He'd passed out and would come back soon – if not right away, then certainly by lunchtime. And then he would open up his doors once again, to begin shaving the men of the village. Later that day, the muhtar had climbed up on to his roof and wandered amongst the piles of dried dung, imagining that he could see Nuri atop the cliffs that rang with eagles' cries, or on the far side of the mournful yellow plain that seemed to grow before his eyes. Going back down, he'd patted a calf's forehead for no reason whatsoever, and later still, on his way to visit Cıngıl Nuri's wife, he'd again let his mind wander: if he were Nuri, and his soul had been reduced to the point of a pin, where might he have gone, leaving behind a wife and three children? The very thought undid him, until there was nothing left inside him but a vast empty space. For forty-two years now, he had bound his eyes, his ears, and even his skin to the spirits of these stones, this soil, this village — to its barking dogs, and stinking dung, and the sharp wind whipping against its grass. And at that moment he'd understood that he'd never go anywhere, even if he wished it. With that, he'd given up on being Nuri. He'd returned to his own body, reclaiming his wrinkled eyes and his tired, lined countenance at just the same moment he'd come face to face with Nuri's wife.

'Where do you think he could have gone?'

The woman had gazed up into the sky for a very long time, apparently relaying the muhtar's question to God, but she'd received no response, or if she did, she'd not understood it. The look on her face had stayed with him; in the years that followed, he had come to believe that he could see in every woman's eyes a void left by men who'd gone missing. He'd look into the eyes of every girl whose breasts had grown to the size of halved apples and, seeing that same void, wondered if it was an absence they all carried from the moment of birth.

They searched everywhere for Nuri that day, asked everyone, without finding a single clue. It was almost as if the man had never existed – as if no one of his name had been the village barber for years on end. Already no one could remember his face; no one could say what kind of nose he'd had, or even if he'd eyes to see with, or a mouth for food and drink. His shop was the only evidence of his ever having existed; even that was under a thickening blanket of dust. There was nothing, nothing at all, to see through the window. The scissors and razors had vanished, the towels and mirrors were nowhere to be seen. Gone, too, was the scent of soap and cologne, except in the minds of those who could remember them.

In those days there were a number of thick-lipped gypsy women who'd go from door to door selling their wares, and when they strapped their bags on their backs and left for neighbouring villages, they carried the news of Nuri's disappearance with them. There was someone who'd said, 'If anyone can find him, they will.' Who this person was, no one could remember. It could have been one of the villagers, or it could have been one of the gypsies. It could have been someone else, someone no one had ever seen or met. It could have been a man with a hairy mole who looked into the far distance, as if his soul were else-where. While according to the women it had been a woman, and who had said anything about looking into the far distance? This woman had looked down at the floor, and said, 'If Nuri can be found, it will be the gypsy women who'll find him.'

So the next time the gypsies' horse-carts rolled back in, the village rose up in hope, racing out to the black tents they'd pitched in the pastures just outside. The women conversed in whispers, beyond the range of the gypsy men with their jaunty hats and great moustaches, until the men of the village took the gypsies off, if not to the coffeehouse, then to their courtyards, to drink the hard stuff. Much wine was drunk in the days that followed, many red-combed cocks lost their lives, and countless henna-stained lambs were roasted. The gypsies' moustaches grew fast and faster, until, after a few days, they were as twisted as the horns of a ram. The swarthy thick-lipped women left their tents to wander through the village, visiting first its streets and its yards, and then its houses, its kitchens, and the shadows of its dowry chests. But still, there was no news from them of Nuri.

Every summer, the villagers' hopes would rise again, when the tinsmith, a crocus curled around his ear, dawdled past on his mangy donkey to set up his stall in the village square. Before the man could so much as jump down from his donkey, the villagers had begun asking of the mountains and valleys he'd crossed and the villages he'd visited, and whether or not he'd heard anything of Nuri. The tinsmith would frown in silence, as if he were trying to juggle his own pots. And for a time the village square would be a sea of sparkling lights, of copper saucepans, pots, spoons and water bowls, all chained together by their handles, until he packed up his stall again and went on his way. He seemed sad; he had been dragged into the fringes of this story of loss, and now he was damned for having had no useful part to play in it. As he left, he said to the watchman, 'I'm going back to where I come from.' The watchman didn't grasp what he meant by this until the tinsmith had gone beyond the mill stream and vanished.

'I suppose the tinsmith lives in many different places,' thought the watchman. Around a week after the tinsmith's departure, a painter with a cylindrical hat was seen by the mill. He and his grey donkey reached the village just as the sun's light was waning. He looked just like his donkey, shivering in the heat and playing with its long ears as he jumped down to gaze at the stream. As they made their way across the pasture, the grey donkey became the painter; it had the cylindrical hat on its head and was blowing cigarette smoke from its mouth. The two walked on for a time, and it seemed as though they would die of exhaustion before they reached the village. They parted at the foot of the plane tree; the painter becoming a painter again, the donkey a donkey. The men sitting outside the village coffeehouse gestured to the painter to sit down, and the donkey, laden with two large cans of paint, wandered over to the mulberry tree where they set up shop every year, and there it stood, flicking its ears soulfully in the way of all donkeys.

No sooner had the painter sat down than they began to ask him about Cıngıl Nuri. As they turned their wooden chairs to face him, they were convinced, for a moment, that he was bringing them news. But the painter just said, 'I've heard he's gone missing.' He could tell them no more. He might not have needed to know a thing, since he had all the village's attention. But the next day, as he was warming his paint, Nuri's wife came with her three children to sit at his side, and she stayed there for some time. The painter told her he had spent the winter painting over weathered woollen carpets, painting them as red as flags, as green as the heavens, as blue as glass beads and as black as dungeons, and in so doing he had painted Nuri into the void.

'I'm going to tell the State. I'll go in and do a missing person's report, so the soldiers and police can start looking for him,' said the muhtar. With that, he mounted his horse and trotted off out of the village. Thereafter, Nuri became a little more lost and his barber shop a little dustier. The villagers spent days awaiting the muhtar's return, watching the road from their rooftops from morning till night. In her dreams Nuri's wife saw the muhtar riding across mountains and plains, highlands and villages; she went to sit on the piles of rocks outside his house, fixing her eyes on the flag flying from the roof. In its bold red and white she saw the mighty gates of the State, and her heart began to pound. She didn't know whether she was frightened or glad: if she was glad, it was a fearful gladness; if she was frightened, it was a happy fear.

Thousands of years later, the muhtar returned from the State, and his voice was as tired as his horse. 'It's done,' he told the woman. 'Everything's done.'

And soon his story spread through the village, exactly as he had told it. He'd knocked on all the State's doors, fixed Nuri's name to every noticeboard, left details in every coffeehouse, inn and restaurant he could find, and if there happened to be a hamam, he'd gone there too. Everyone knew everything now: everyone had a share in Nuri's absence. All that was left was to wait in silence for the red-winged bird of good tidings to swoop down from the skies. If not today, then tomorrow. Hearing these words Nuri's wife was almost as elated as if her husband had been found. She ran back to her children, crying long and hard, throwing her arms around them and kissing them a hundred times over. Every day, she went back to the muhtar's house to sit on those rock piles outside it and stare up at the flag. But now she could see the gates of the State more clearly. Sometimes, as she sat in their shadow, the worry returned, and she needed to lean forward to get a better look. There was a great hall behind those gates, and it was plunged in darkness. Long-faced scribes were seated around a long table writing out her husband's name. Their hands held pens as long as shepherds' staffs, which caught the light as they scribbled. Then seals were affixed to the papers, seals many times bigger than the muhtar's. Gigantic seals, the grandfathers of all seals, with stamps that cast long, long shadows. Then the papers were slipped into envelopes, to be placed ceremoniously into the pockets of sharp-faced messengers. Yet one of the envelopes was forgotten, left in the room to crackle as the messengers departed. Fearing that this might be the envelope bearing Nuri's name, his wife took several steps forward to stand in the path of the muhtar as he left his house.

The muhtar had said that Nuri would come today or tomorrow.

Again, the door creaked open. The cat licked itself. Its tongue called to mind a red handkerchief.

'Reşit's still waiting,' said the muhtar's wife. 'Aren't you coming?'

The muhtar took off his vomit-stained undershirt and threw it at the wall.

'I'm coming,' he shouted angrily. 'Wait!'

5

When the barber turned from the street to the man with the goatee who sat waiting in the chair, his eyes still carried the glint of the executioner's blade.

'Your hair has grown into your beard,' he said, in a voice that cast a veil over those eyes.

The man with the goatee said nothing. He just sat there, eyes shut, as if he feared seeing himself in the mirror. It was almost as if he was not the one whose hair had grown into his beard; as if part of him was living in another place, a place no one had ever heard of, while the rest of him sat dozing in this chair. But when the barber's scissors started clicking, he woke up.

'Cut the moustache so there's no more hair going into my mouth, and stop there,' he said, as he stared up at the charcoal sketch of the dove above the mirror. 'Did you draw that picture?'

'Yes, I did, and you've asked me this before,' replied the barber. 'Every time you come in here, you ask me.'

The man with the goatee shrank into himself like a scolded child, as he lowered his gaze to the mirror. The apprentice went behind the curtain at the back of the shop; returning with a broom, he began to sweep up the hair on the floor.

'Leave it,' said the man with the goatee. 'Leave it!'

The barber's apprentice froze; wide-eyed, he watched the man rise from his seat. It wasn't clear who he was talking to.

The man rushed to the door. Before plunging into the crowded street, he turned around.

'The money's run out,' he said to the barber. 'It's full of skeletons out there.'

The barber shook his head. He watched sadly as the man with the goatee hurtled across the pavement. He kept his eyes on him until he had zigzagged through the traffic to vanish around the corner. It was as if this man's departure had deflated him somehow.

'Who was that?' I asked timidly.

'His name's Nuri,' said the barber. 'I have no idea who he is, or where he's from.'

6

As he slowly buttoned up his shirt, the muhtar gazed with tired eyes out of the window: the village lay under the sun like a white wounded animal. It seemed to be breathing its last breath, its shiver passing through every house and every street. And now he could hear the squeak of an ox-cart, as a flock of chirping sparrows rose up from the mulberry tree. Then the flock divided down the middle, with the first half diving fast as rain towards who-knows-whose courtyard, and the second flying straight up to Cıngıl Nuri's house.

Back then, they'd gathered at Nuri's house for a meeting. It was evening. In the hope, perhaps, that they might guide Nuri home, his wife had lit two candles in the corner of each room. Their smoke rose in spirals to the corncobs hanging from the ceiling. Nuri's relatives, meanwhile, were sitting side by side on the divan. From time to time, the old men stroked their beards in consternation, while others stared at the candles, thinking deep thoughts. Some clicked their prayer beads with an impatience which suggested that any problem under the sun could be solved just as fast.

As Nuri's wife saw it, the muhtar wasn't taking this business seriously enough: he'd just handed the matter over to the State and washed his hands of it. He hadn't bothered to keep in touch with the district headquarters. He hadn't even asked that a barber be sent from a neighbouring village to take over the shop that Nuri had abandoned. Whatever needed doing, they needed to do themselves, and that was why they had decided to go back to the beginning and reach a proper agreement.

The men on the divan listened solemnly as the woman spoke, and then they shook their heads. Each time they moved, the shadows they cast on the wall grew longer, until suddenly they shrank. It was almost as if these shadows were conversing with each other, almost as if they were searching for another Nuri in another world.

The meeting lasted until the rooster's first crow. The children curled up along the walls and slept as their white-bearded elders held forth. One of their number began by offering examples from the past – naming names unknown to them in death, as in life. A few nodded in agreement. Then another old man repeated the same stories, but in greater detail. The rest fell into line, following his crackling voice into the distant past. Soon they were amongst their own grandfathers. But it didn't last long, this return to their history's most secret page. Before long, the crackling voice was rounding them all up. Returned to the room, they gazed at each other in terror. For they could see in each other the bloody tally of the secrets that Nuri's disappearance might reveal.

Towards dawn, they drifted home, each one quivering like notes plucked from the morning call to prayer. Leaving the half-lit streets behind them, they lay down to a troubled sleep. They rose with the birds, of course. Whereupon some downed a glass of mountain tea, and some did not, before packing their saddlebags with bread, cheese and underwear and setting out to find Nuri.

The muhtar sent them off with a stern warning: should they pass through the city, on no account were they to call at district headquarters to ask about Nuri. There was no need to waste the State's time: its functionaries could be merciless with those who did. The State was the State, and so not to be bothered. Upset the State in any way, and it would persist in what it had been doing for fifteen years now, which was to refuse to acknowledge their village even existed. And that was why they should on no account knock on the doors of the State. It was fully aware of the situation, and the bulletin boards of every quarter had been fully bulleted – they could be sure of that. Instead they should concentrate on ordinary people. They should ask after Nuri at restaurants and hotels, coffeehouses and hamams. And barber shops, of course: Nuri being a barber, other barbers might have a way of sniffing him out. And anyway, barbers were men who thrived on chatter: they kept their eyes and ears peeled. They missed nothing. And one more thing: when they asked after Nuri, they should not describe him as he was on the day he disappeared. So many years had passed since then, so much could have changed. They could be sure he would not still be wearing the same shirt; his nose might have changed in shape – his mouth, too; his hair might be longer and his beard fuller; even his gaze might have changed. And that could be the reason why they'd not yet found him.

The men nodded in agreement. Mounting their horses and their donkeys, they gazed with weak hope at the mountains beyond the plain, their shoulders already sagging with the fatigue they would carry home with them.

Weeks passed, and months, and endless years. Every two or three months, the searchers would send a telegram, which a district postman would deliver by motorbike. First he would circle the plane tree in the village square, ignoring everyone he passed. Rising mournfully from the great cloud of dust, he would ask for the muhtar, and with these words he would send the entire village into mad anticipation. The fields would empty as crowds congregated in the village square. These postmen never stayed long, though: as soon as they had delivered the telegram they would leap back on to their motorbikes and, after doing another loop around the plane tree, disappear. It was almost as if they feared taking the blame for what had happened to Nuri and wished to escape before the latest news spread. They did not even glance over their shoulders as they fled. For months afterwards, the children would play in the tracks they left, puttering like motorcycles as they ran circles around the plane tree. Usually, it was Cennet's son who chased them home. He would charge at them, as if he were a child himself, despite his great size, and send them scattering.

In the muhtar's opinion, these telegrams brought nothing but disappointment. With the commotion they caused, the village would have been better off getting no telegrams at all. Because sometimes a new telegram would contradict all the telegrams that had come before; sometimes the last word would undermine the first word so as to leave a telegram's true meaning entirely in doubt. The village was left not knowing what to believe. In time, it was left to the night watchman to decipher their hidden meanings. Because he read each telegram many hundreds of times. Nuri's wife began to treat every telegraph as though it were a part of her husband's body. She would hide them between her breasts, until, on a whim, she sauntered off to the watchman to have him read them out to her.

A good three years had passed by the time the searchers returned from wherever on earth they had been all that while, with their lined foreheads, sagging shoulders, and shrivelled hopes. They said not a word: it was as if they'd not been away all those years, and not seen a thing, or if they had gone somewhere, they'd come back as other people. Or maybe they'd left part of themselves behind – maybe that's why they were so taciturn and distant. Nuri's wife was at her wits' end. She raced from house to house, flapping her arms, chasing after answers like a chicken chasing newly hatched chicks.

But in the end, it was the village's new barber who brought the first news of Nuri. This was the year Gıcır Hamza got a chickpea stuck in his nose; the villagers were still talking about how much the chickpea had swollen, and how, in his violent efforts to blow that chickpea out through his other nostril, and falling to the ground, he had also expelled a dead fly. That same year, the muhtar had given up trying to run the village from his house. And on that particular day, he was in the village square, working on the barn that was to become his office. He had taken down the flagpole that had once graced his own roof and planted it in front. It had been rumoured that deputies from the National Assembly would be making a visit that day to discuss digging irrigation canals on the plain, though the muhtar himself had received no official confirmation. He had, in fact, received nothing in writing from the men in high places since first being elected muhtar, but he still wanted to be ready for them, just in case they chose that day to make their appearance.

The watchman was sitting out in front. Stretched before him was a length of linen on which he was painting the slogan that the muhtar had, after long deliberation, deemed suitable: *Our Village Is Grateful to You.* His hands were now painted red up to the wrists; he looked, for all the world, like a murderer with blood on his hands, guarding the muhtar's doors.

It was at this very moment that the barber arrived. Rounding the creek next to the mill, he was nothing more than a tall and blurry shadow shimmering in the heat; at first glance, he could have been anything, but as he came closer it became clear that he was human, whereupon the villagers gathered in the shade of the plane tree began to crane their necks. But he must have sensed the stir he was causing, because he was walking very slowly. You might even say that he going around in circles, staring and stopping, and sometimes even hopping one step back, so that by the time he reached the village square, many hours had passed, and though they didn't show it, the villagers had lost patience. The barber, by contrast, was exceedingly calm. Having at last set down his suitcase, he found himself a chair. His face was drawn, as if there were a second face attached to it – a face made from a mixture of skin and bones and dirt, which glowed, now and again, like a dusty mirror lost in time. The watchman, recalling the crooked lettering of his banner, reached for his rifle with his blood-red hands. Placing it between his legs, he planted himself in front of the barber. There was something odd, he thought, about a man who could just turn up like this, holding just one suitcase, and then keep himself to himself by stubbornly responding to questions with the shortest possible answer. Could he be a scout, he wondered, sent in advance by the deputies from the National Assembly? Was he here to give them a thorough inspection, before submitting his report?

Through narrowed eyes, he looked the man over. It was almost as if he'd grown up in this village; his ears seemed untouched by the swaying of the plane tree, his eyes by the white heat rising from the rooftops, his skin by the furiously burning soil. Perhaps this was why the watchman was the only one that day who did find him unsettling. The others picked up where he had left off. Some of the old men were skilled at guiding a conversation in the direction they desired, and never so much as when they were conversing with a stranger. They kept giving him openings, and then pulling back. But still the man would not talk. Their questions rose up unanswered into the branches of the plane tree, until the shoemaker lost his temper:

'Where exactly did you come from?' he asked. 'And where are you going?' The man's face fell, or rather, his real face slipped into his second, earthen face. 'I'm a barber,' he said. 'I come from afar. Across lands already forgotten . . .'

Upon hearing these words, the village square fell silent. A few moments passed, and the muhtar sat down next to the man. Prayer beads snapping, the muhtar ordered him a glass of tea and, knowing that a barber was best placed to follow the scent of another barber, asked him if he'd seen Nuri.

'I knew someone called Nuri,' said the barber. 'His hair had grown into his beard. A tiny little man. Every once in a while, he'd come to me for a shave.'

The villagers were stunned by these words: they moved not an eyelash. It wasn't long before the news had reached Nuri's wife at home. When she ran into the village square, she found the barber still sitting with the muhtar. For a moment, their eyes met; the woman looked at the barber, the barber at the woman. The barber seemed secretly guilty, almost. Though the watchman was squatting some distance away, he could read this in the man's face. He looked at him again, through narrowed eyes, and churning doubt. Nuri's wife was as shocked and tearful as if she were standing face to face with her husband. Fearing that she might fall to the ground to cling to the barber's feet, the muhtar took her by the arms and sat her down. 'This is Nuri's wife,' he told the barber.

The barber looked at her as though he'd known her for forty years. In his eyes, there was first the glint of an executioner's blade, and then nothing. For a moment, the shoemaker wondered if this man before them could actually be Nuri. 'What if Nuri abandoned every familiar part of him somewhere far away,' he asked himself, 'to return to the village in a different guise?'

The woman had fixed her mournful eyes upon the barber. She was waiting for him to start from the beginning, and explain everything. But the barber did not say another word. It was left to the muhtar to calm her down. The two men shared a name, he told her, but there the similarity ended. It wasn't clear how far she believed him; she just sat there staring at the barber. It was almost as if she had made a connection with this man, succeeding where all others, apart from the shoemaker, had failed. This may explain why, when the muhtar suggested that the barber stay on in the village, she immediately offered Nuri's old shop. He could use it, she said, until Nuri returned.

'So it's agreed?' the muhtar asked.

Without saying a word, the barber nodded.

And now it all came back: the string of preposterous rumours that had followed on from this agreement. Only yesterday, there'd been a pedlar, claiming to have seen Nuri driving a blue truck. This was impossible. Even Nuri's wife could not imagine it: this was a man who struggled to keep hold of the reins of his own donkey. However would he manage with an enormous truck? She ran straight to the village square, to tell the pedlar he must be wrong, but when she got there, he was gone. In actual fact, no one in the village could tell her when this pedlar had arrived or departed. The watchman had gone so far as to whip his rifle out from underneath his chair and race out to the mill, but he'd seen no one either.

The muhtar and Nuri's wife had both been in the village square that day, along with the shoemaker, Rıza the shopkeeper, and a few others. Cennet's son kept insisting that he'd seen the pedlar, telling anyone who doubted his word he'd swear it on the Koran. Gıcır Hamza did the same, insisting over and over that he was prepared to put his hand on the Koran and say he'd seen the pedlar at the coffeehouse around mid-morning: they'd even sat down in the coffeehouse together, to chat over a glass of tea.

The watchman was not convinced. To his mind, the pedlar could not be just a pedlar. Most probably, he was a scout, sent by the deputies from the National Assembly. Who could know what he'd discovered before disappearing, or what he'd write in his report?

Perhaps he'd come to the village to spread the news that Cıngıl Nuri was now driving a truck: perhaps this had been his sole mission. Perhaps he'd been lumbered with this task for months now, growing ever wearier under its weight; which had, in the end, become so very heavy that, after delivering the news, he'd risen up into the air, as light as a baby chick's feather, and floated off. He'd left a great lie behind him. For it was clear now that the State had devised this lie so as to remove all trace of Nuri; he must have been long dead. But somehow, he'd been registered as a driver, and driving was what he now did. Day and night, he was on the road, as tired as the sleepless roads themselves. No one would ever know where he was at this moment, or where he might be a little later, or where he had been a while before. He carried his house upon his back; wherever he was, wherever he was headed, he made that place his home. And that was why, when the State set about inventing a likely alibi for the man, it had chosen to make him a driver – this was a job without an address! The State wanted to make sure the villagers never found him, while continuing to believe he was alive.

All well and good – but what had made Nuri so important as to require elimination? This the watchman didn't know. He might well have been the first victim of a campaign of eliminations that would last until the end of time. The State might well have said, 'Let's eliminate one person from each village.' Nuri might have been its test case, in preparation for the challenges ahead. And the pedlar who had vanished, faster than a ghost – well, who could be sure he wasn't sitting on the other side of those mountains, sketching their faces from memory. Saying: this is what they look like. These are their eyes, their noses and their mouths; this is the shape of their faces and the size of their homes. This is the plane tree in the village square, and this is the muhtar, standing next to it. This is Rıza the shopkeeper. Next to him Cennet's son, and next along is Reşit . . .

But the barber was nowhere to be found in this crowd. Instead he was standing at his shop door, staring. In the shoemaker's opinion, he was a monster of silence, an interloper who had stolen Nuri's shop and livelihood; unless he was another Nuri, dressed in different clothes – a Nuri who nursed a grudge against everyone and everything in the whole wide world. When the imam turned up in the village square that day, he had fixed him, no doubt, with the same stare.

The imam, meanwhile, saw nothing. He was bent over double, so much so that his nose scraped the ground as he walked. Only when he had joined the crowd did he straighten up to fix the muhtar with his penetrating gaze. Nuri's wife jumped forward to tell him what had happened, until the muhtar silenced her with a single sweep of the hand.

'Let's not make things any more complicated than they already are,' he barked. 'Let me do the explaining!'

This he did, and the longer he spoke, the straighter the imam stood, and the more gravely he shook his head. His eyes searched the crowd, stopping from time to time to cast suspicion on Cennet's son and

Gıcır Hamza. Then he started muttering. It wasn't clear what he was saying, but it was clear from his furrowed eyebrows that he was angry.

Suddenly he bellowed, 'Are you mad? No pedlar has come to this village in years!'

Now everyone was shocked. Even the children who had chased after the pedlar were shocked. The shock passed through them to combine with the elements. In the time it might take to crack a whip, almost, the atmosphere changed. Now villagers shuddered at the very sight of each other, as if they'd seen a ghost. They wandered the streets like sleepwalkers; they heard no words that were not uttered twice. Even the streets tied themselves up into knots, turning and tangling and looping back on themselves. Front doors seemed to shrink, as nooks and crannies multiplied, and courtyards silently widened. Half of everything was lost, and half the time not even a broom could be found. A spade in the corner of the courtyard would pick itself up to hide itself behind the piled sacks of chickpeas. Spoons and trays and pots would go missing, only to turn up months later in a neighbour's house. Even the chickens seemed no longer to know if they were chickens, or something else. The trees, meanwhile, crossed over into the animal kingdom. Sometimes, when a flower opened, it lowed like a cow, or bleated like a sheep. A clump of wisteria might suddenly leap across the courtyard to fly down the street. Even the muhtar – he who thought that he ought to be the last person in the village to be shocked – was shocked. Every time he made love to his wife – even as he stripped off his clothes – the imam's words came back to him. And there it would end: the kissing and caressing. The moment would be lost. Shrinking back into himself, he would fix his eyes on the wall. His wife attributed this behaviour to Ethem's daughter Gülcan; every time her husband caught sight of the girl, he shivered from head to toe. This had been going on for a year now. The girl's budding breasts had dazzled, even crippled, the man.

Thank God he had his position to think of. He was intimately connected to every family in the village. So of course he was beholden to them – to the white-bearded old men, to the babies and their sky-blue beads, to his friends and his neighbours, the wolves in the mountains and the birds in the trees, not to mention his own future and good name. Had it been otherwise, nothing – not even prophets raining down from the heavens – would have stopped him. For as long as the man had breath in his body, he would have chased after her, until those sighing lips and budding breasts were his. And yes, maybe he was fretting about Nuri just a little, but even so, there was also this girl. He'd taken to leaving his sentences half-finished. He'd ask a question and then wander off before anyone could answer. And of course, from time to time, he'd lose himself in his thoughts. Now that the repairs to the muhtar's office were finished, there were days when he sat all alone there, from dawn to dusk, staring at the walls.

Happening as it did so soon after his election, Nuri's disappearance preyed on him. He had no idea how to behave. As much as he wanted to pluck Nuri out of whatever hell he was in, and hand him over to his wife and children, he knew it was his duty to bring calm to the village, no matter what the price. But they had all been thrown off course; before anyone even had the chance to comment on the latest rumour, it would be replaced by another. It was almost as if a host of alien creatures had descended on the village as it slept, to sprinkle the mulberry trees and the roosters' tails and the court-yard gates with a thousand and one rumours. They'd feed on the darkness like leeches, and by morning they'd have taken on the aura of truth. And in the morning, when the village rose from its slumbers, it would meet these rumours before it met itself. And it would recoil in shock, in ignorance of the darkness that had nourished these untruths, caught between belief and the thought that there was nothing left to believe in.

This was what happened when the village heard that Nuri had gone to Germany. For a time no dog barked, no cock crowed and no horse whinnied. In every orchard and garden, they were telling the story of how Nuri had crossed over the border. They seemed to know every detail, from the size of his suitcase to the stripes on his shirt, from the shine of his shoes to the smile on his face. The only thing they didn't know was who had seen all this, but hardly anyone wondered what this might mean; caught up in the torrent of tiny details, they were blinded, with no time to ask.

Then came the news that Nuri had won the lottery. This prompted his relatives to call for another search party, but the muhtar managed to talk them out of it. There was no need; if Nuri wanted to be found, he'd come back on his own two feet. If he wanted to stay hidden, there was no hope of ever finding him. If they set out yet again to find him, they would, meanwhile, feel the loss all the more keenly.

Truth be told, Nuri's wife could not fathom the muhtar's logic. Just the thought of all those other women who had spent her husband's money was enough to send her into hysterics. In time, all the other women in the neighbourhood would flock to her house. Together they would slap their knees and wail. So wild were those wails that the imam could no longer climb his wooden minaret knowing that his voice would be heard far and wide. No man could rest his head on his pillow, or sit down in the coffeehouse and string two words together in the confidence that he would be understood. But equally, no one could find the heart to have a word with Nuri's wife.

When they heard that the deputies they had been expecting for so long had left for the capital, the women suddenly stopped wailing. It was when they were taking down the banner on which the muhtar and watchman had spent a thousand and one labours. News came that Nuri's wife had locked herself into her house. At once the muhtar sent over his wife for an eyewitness report. If she had locked herself in, exactly how had she done so? And where were the children? Were they, too, condemned to this fate?

In a flash, his wife was back at his side. It was an utter disaster: the woman had nailed all the doors and windows shut. She wouldn't let her uncle in, or her father.

Those little lambs were inside, too, bleating away. Not a sound from their mother. No one knew if there was so much as a crumb of bread in the house, or water.

'Let's just leave her to it,' said the muhtar. 'Let the woman do what she has to do, and maybe she'll calm down.'

But the stubborn woman kept it going longer than he expected. Every two days or so, the watchman would walk around the house, staring at the windows. Inside, it was as silent as a grave.

In a mumble worthy of a Koranic verse, he said, 'What this house needs is Nuri.'

With that, he raised his rifle and set out for the muhtar's office.

Three weeks later, at the insistence of both the muhtar and the imam, Nuri's door finally opened. Everyone in the village was there to watch; the rooftops and the courtyards were teeming with people, and there were more lining the walls of nearby houses. Even the dogs came to watch. Boys watched from their doorways, catapults hanging from their necks, their eyes so wide you would think they expected a flock of sparrows to come surging out in one great rush. They were dry-mouthed, every last one of them. Somewhere in the crowd were women saying that there was a dead child inside. The news spread in whispers, until everyone stood ready for the chill of death. The muhtar and the imam lingered at the door, tapping on the window from time to time, speaking to someone inside. Giving up, they would return to the crowd, shaking their heads. But soon they would be running back to the door, looking hopeful. Whenever they did that, the villagers would fall silent: even the ones who'd been talking about a dead child fell silent, and spoke with their eyes instead. The muhtar hid his anger from the woman inside, but the crowd outside could see his anger in every sweep of his hand. Then suddenly children looked up at the sky. And there, through the parting clouds, came an aeroplane; a shiny, metal bird . . . Soaring high in the sky, beyond the reach of stones and catapults, and in its wake it left a trail of smoke as long as Nuri's wife was stubborn.

Slowly, the door opened.

'Reşit is losing his patience,' said the muhtar's wife. 'Are you coming down or not?'

The muhtar nodded as he bent over to pull on his socks. Caressed by the sweet aroma of aniseed, he left the room. Reşit was waiting with his hands in his lap, silent and resigned as a disciple. First they exchanged greetings. Then the muhtar had a foreboding; a whiff of something bad. It was, he thought, like the moment before an explosion, the moment before everything around him shattered. The greenflies would start buzzing; they'd buzz louder and louder, until, with a great clap of thunder, the greatest the living world had ever known, they succumbed to an unholy din. Until they had sent tense, tight fire trails crackling across the sky, defying the line between this world and the next. Meanwhile, they all braced themselves: the ox-cart wheels in the courtyards, iron-ringed cattle, the walls, the shadows of the mulberry trees and the sky. They braced themselves against the growing hum.

The muhtar looked back at the village. He looked back because he was afraid, as afraid as he'd been during his first days as muhtar. He couldn't remember exactly when, but just after he was elected for the third time, three people had died on the same day. One was a young shepherd – a child, almost. He'd fallen while trying to take dove eggs from a nook in the cliffs. His head had been dashed to pieces, scattering bits of his brain across the ground, like yoghurt. The next was a widower who had eaten mushrooms: one minute he was standing outside the coffeehouse, the picture of health. The next moment he was a large and foaming mouth in a revolving head. The third death bore no resemblance to any death he'd ever heard of; a seventeen-year-old girl, who, in the hope of assuaging some unknown pain, had affixed two whole bottles of leeches to her body before retiring to bed. As she slept, the leeches ballooned with blood, until all that remained was a pile of yellow meat.

'So,' said the muhtar, 'what's wrong, Reşit?'

Reşit swallowed. Hat in hand, he looked straight into the muhtar's eyes.

'Güvercin the Dove has disappeared,' he whispered, as if from the depths of a canyon. 'She's gone. Lost.'

7

Then it was time for the man with the prayer beads that were as black as dungeons. He rose slowly, as if it were not a chair awaiting him, but his own execution. The barber's apprentice stood ready with a yellow-and-white-striped towel. But the man didn't see this, nor did he wish to see it. He just plumped himself into a chair, in defiance of his executioner. It was clear that he loathed being shaved.

The barber moistened his brush with hot water and rubbed it on the soap until it lathered. I held my breath, transfixed. His hands moved so fast that they, and the soap, looked as if they weren't moving at all. As if they had turned to ice, almost. And maybe the barber had turned to ice with them, and with the man in the chair, and me . . . It seemed as if we were all living somewhere else in that moment, in a different time, and a different place. It was as if we were, without knowing it, just imagining that we were here. Together we let out a deep sigh. And perhaps this was because, in that other place, we were caught up in some endless struggle. Perhaps, in that other place, we were grappling with all manner of things; running, shouting, ranting, drenched in sweat, but never with a moment to rest. Perhaps that was why we had all turned to ice. Perhaps, when we began to move again in this place, in that other, faraway and unknowable place, we would turn to ice.

Suddenly, the barber's hands stopped moving; or rather, they began moving again. It was almost as if I could see both places at once: this one here, and the one so far away. In one everything was moving; in the other everything had turned to ice. They merged, these visions, and then they drew apart.

'Put the blade on the razor,' said the barber.

The apprentice extracted the blade they'd used for Nuri and threw it into a plastic bucket under the counter. And now the man in the chair had a face of white foam, though the barber was still turning his brush to daub on more. It was almost as if he'd got carried away; with his left hand he held the man's forehead like a vice, as with his right hand he lathered on soap with something that looked like an unbridled lust. There was even soap hanging like earrings from the man's earlobes now.

'Master,' said the apprentice. 'We've run out of razor blades.'

The barber stopped lathering, but his brush was still on the man's cheek.

'Run!' he shouted. 'Buy five boxes at least. Make sure they're Perma-Sharp!'

With that, the apprentice vanished.

8

The barber had pulled his chair up to the window. And there he sat, unblinking. The kettle behind the curtain had not come to a boil; but he was sure he'd hear it bubble any moment now. It had become something of a habit: leaving his seat by the window from time to time, to brew up some tea, returning with a huge glass to drink while he stared out at the village square. The tea helped, somehow; glancing at the mirror, he could see its sour taste reflected. And it took him away from the clouds gathering with such menace beyond that mirror, and from his own understanding.

He put down his glass and stood up. That same moment he noticed the divan saz on the wall, and the two flies strolling between its seven strings, seeking respite, perhaps, from their own relentless buzzing, while trying to memorise all the folk songs that these quivering strings could play. Just then, the kettle behind the curtain came to a boil; as he took it off the hob, the barber wondered how he had come to be thinking about these buzzing flies. He was fearful, almost, of the flies in his mind falling into the water boiling before his eyes, and so, while he was waiting for the tea to brew, he ceded to that other barber, still lurking inside the saz, and the flies launched into a new tune. Their wings shuddered as they struggled to keep time, but as the barber returned to his chair, the presence inside the saz fell silent. The flies dropped to the floor, only to buzz back into the air.

Just then, he caught sight of the muhtar. He was striding across the village square. Behind him was Reşit and his hunched shadow. The man was in a panic. He looked like he was going to curl up in the dust like a bug. The muhtar, for his part, was playing the muhtar better than ever; from his calm and measured steps, it was clear that he was seething.

He did not say a word until he reached the scene of the crime. He looked straight through those who greeted him as he passed. He ignored the red creepers that caused him to stumble, and the drifting heads of barley grass, and the four children who were trying to mount a foal they'd just captured. Entering Reşit's courtyard, the muhtar stopped short, like a general, to sniff the air. It was almost as if he expected to find something hidden under the horse-cart, or the woodpile, or the wire mesh with the broken frame, the pickaxe lying on its side, or the shovel, or the wings of the chickens wandering around the coop. They were like people hiding secrets, these things – trying to act natural, trying not to stand out.

'Gone without a trace,' said Reşit.

The muhtar subjected the courtyard to another inspection. It was his belief that everything must surely leave a trace: without a trace, there was nothing. Even birds left their mark on the sky, as did words on teeth. Give someone a look, and you could see it etched on their face. It was almost as if Güvercin the Dove had never gone up those wooden stairs, had never left the feed bowl in front of the coop, or leant against the cartwheel on a sunny day to do her lace-work, or pressed her nose against the window and sighed, or dangled her hair out of the window to look out on to the road: every trace of her had disappeared. There must be traces of her somewhere, or at least the traces of whoever it was who had stolen her away . . . There was too much surface detail, and perhaps, beneath that detail, there was a hidden vault. An empty space, even.

The muhtar searched Reşit's eyes. He searched for an empty space, an empty space large enough for Güvercin to flutter her wings and take flight. He found nothing. 'It must be only in women's glances that you can find empty spaces like that,' he thought, remembering Cıngıl Nuri's wife. He walked over to the far end of the courtyard. Wherever he went, Reşit followed. But silently, and trying not to overtake him. It was almost as if he thought that before Güvercin could be found, all of the dogs of the village would have to stop barking, and the children complaining, and the cartwheels creaking. Only when the village felt silent would she let down her golden locks and make her way home. And that was why, as he tiptoed up the stairs behind the muhtar, he glanced up at a top-floor window, only to catch a glimpse of his wife crying. She couldn't see them, as it happened; her eyes were downcast and her eyelashes moist. Her only thoughts were for her lost girl, as she sobbed through gritted teeth. It was as if she were lost, too. She seemed not to know she was sitting at the window, even.

When she heard the door open she turned her head to see a dishevelled old man standing next to her husband. For a moment, she couldn't place him, but when she realised he was the muhtar, she put her head in her hands and began to wail. The wails rose in volume, as the muhtar scanned the room, as if to keep something from flitting away beyond his grasp. Then he squatted on the floor to inspect each and every colour in the carpets. He passed his hands over the curtains, to see whether the creases were fake or real. He went to the window to contemplate the view, compared the distance between the ground and window with the greatest height he could imagine a human leaping, and when all that was done, he ambled to the door with a furtive, knowing grin, so as to mask his disappointment at having found nothing.

'Is her trousseau still here?' he asked.

'It's all still here,' said Reşit.

'So was she in love with anyone, or anyone with her?'

'I don't know.'

Returning to the courtyard, they walked out to the cherry trees behind the house.

'Of course you don't know. Did you ask her mother?'

'I did. She doesn't know either.'

As they stood together in the shade, the muhtar looked back at the house. He conjured up the dimly lit rooms behind those adobe walls, and the croaking rusty doors, the soot-black hearths, the bags of chickpeas piled high and Reşit's wife's sobs. He took a few steps back. Then, as if escaping an unseen danger, he rushed out of the courtyard and vanished. Abandoned with so little notice, Reşit was at a loss, caught between wanting to go inside to shout at his wife and wanting to go after the muhtar.

Once again, the barber looked through the window and saw the muhtar. He was no longer hiding his panic:

it was now there for all to see. The visor of his cap was turned upwards. In his hand were his amber prayer beads. He was kicking something across the ground, but that something wasn't there. Resting his head on his hands, the barber fixed his executioner's eyes on the village square. At that moment he saw a pair of feet coming straight towards him. He knew that gait well, and the properties attached to it (jaunty, but also very sad, and lazy in the way it carried its owner, and forlorn at being passed over, but also taking pride in every last stone or insect it encountered).

'That's the shoemaker,' he thought.

He looked up; indeed, it was he. His arms were swaying at his sides so helplessly that the barber almost wanted to cry. But he didn't: fearful of seeing things differently from everyone else, he preferred to think that nothing ever made sense. The shoemaker walked in, hiding his thoughts behind a smile as worn as the soles of his own shoes.

'Did you hear what happened?' he asked, sitting himself down.

'I heard,' said the barber, 'Güvercin has gone missing.'

The shoemaker looked shocked.

'Who did you hear that from?' he asked.

The barber did not reply. His eyes had travelled elsewhere, as he sat there, still as a stone.

9

When the watchman came rushing into the muhtar's office, he found him bent over his desk, chain-smoking and staring at his official seal. When the door opened, he seemed not to notice. When it closed, he remained just as still. If it weren't for the smoke pouring from his mouth, the watchman would have had no way of knowing if he was still breathing.

For many long hours, the watchman stood there waiting, shifting his weight from foot to foot. As the silence continued, he decided that his next task was going to be very difficult. With this in mind, he tried to straighten his posture, suck in his stomach, and puff up his chest. And then, to stop his eyes from wandering, he stared at a fixed point on the wall in front of him, in the manner of a statue of an unknown soldier, blankly compelling a general to cast aside his doubts and fight to the death.

The muhtar watched him in silence, through the shimmering clouds of blue smoke.

'Sit down,' he said, suddenly.

The watchman sat down. As he wedged his rifle between his knees, he realised that the muhtar had no assignment for him. He had called him here for help.

The muhtar swallowed a few times before saying, 'Now think. Think carefully.'

The watchman had no idea what he was supposed to think about.

Then the muhtar asked, 'Who in this village could kidnap a girl?'

Squeezing the rifle between his knees, the watchman looked down at the floor. He imagined himself leaving the muhtar's office and walking towards the village square. Arriving at the plane tree, he stopped to look right, and then left. There, at his window, the barber was sitting alone, drinking tea. 'He's an odd one,' thought the watchman. 'No one even knows where he came from . . . Or if he's married or not . . . Even so this barber doesn't have it in him to kidnap a girl. Wherever would he hide her? It's only a few square metres, that shop of his. It's not even a proper shop. Half of it's a house . . .'

He turned his attention to other houses, searching each window for clues that might help him answer the muhtar's question. He cast his eyes over each door, each chimney and courtyard. But every time he glanced over his shoulder, there was the barber. So he went back. The barber was still drinking tea in silence. His eyes were fixed on the street to the left of the plane tree. Following the man's strange gaze, the watchman turned left. And there was Cennet's son; he was walking up to the top of the village waving some string above his head. Seeing this, the watchman dived into a side street. He seemed to be running away from something, this boy. He looked upset, but at the same time enlivened by the chase. He kept hopping out of view, like a flea. Then he started peeking into each courtyard he passed. He began to laugh, and each time he did, he emitted a cloud of grey smoke, as a cigarette stub lolled in his mouth, like a second tongue.

'I'm waiting,' said the muhtar.

Keeping his eyes on the floor, and speaking in a low voice, the watchman said, 'I'm thinking.'

That angered the muhtar, though he continued to wait in silence.

Returning to his daydream, the watchman resumed his search. And now he had walked up as far as Cıngıl Nuri's house. Cennet's son was there somewhere. He came to a full stop. And then, with little clipped steps, he twirled around, to take in the fields, the orchards, the harvested chickpeas, and the ditches.

'Have you had a good think now?' asked the muhtar.

'I have.'

'And who comes to mind?'

'Cennet's son!'

The muhtar leant back and looked into the watchman's eyes. Then he stood up. Furiously, he began to pace the room.

'Don't let him out of your sight,' he said. 'Follow him wherever he goes!'

'So who is he supposed to have kidnapped?' asked the watchman.

'Reşit's daughter.'

'Güvercin the Dove?'

The muhtar nodded. The watchman nodded, too, and he kept on nodding, as his face grew longer.

'Go now, and take a look at Cennet's son. Find out where he is and what he's doing. Once you've done that, send for Mustafa and Ramazan, so we can find out what they think!'

The watchman threw his rifle over his shoulder and set off.

Calling after him, the muhtar said, 'Tell them to come with their horses!'

Then – as if to keep from being crushed by a burden too heavy for any man to carry – he collapsed into his chair. Whatever this burden was, it did not stop him standing up now and again to peer through the window. The truth of the matter was that he was afraid. Afraid of Güvercin's sudden disappearance, afraid of the silence that had fallen over the village, and afraid of all that would follow it. The village had succumbed to despair, that much was clear. But he had no idea where this despair had come from, or what it meant. Whatever he saw, it impeded his view of what he really needed to see: it was the same with everything he touched, or tasted. What he resented most of all was that this despair carried no meaning; it was something that just descended on him, every time he was elected muhtar.

Hearing the pounding of horses' hooves, he returned to his desk. The horses halted at his door and whinnied.

The muhtar threw his hat across the table.

'Güvercin's vanished,' he said to the men walking through the door, 'I have no idea how. Some devil must have gone and snatched her. So now I want you to each set off in opposite directions, to as many villages as your horses can take you . . . Ask every living soul you meet along the way if they've seen two shadows flitting past, or a girl on her own. Don't forget that any muhtars you meet were elected or re-elected yesterday, just like me. So you must not forget to convey my congratulations.

Come on to the subject gently. Ask if any strangers have come through the village recently. Don't forget to ask shepherds – they may have seen or heard something, too.'

When Mustafa and Ramazan left the muhtar's office, they came face to face with the entire village. The men and the boys had crowded around the door, to stare inside. The women behind them were struggling to restrain their tears with moans as thin as lace. That was all that could be heard, in any event: the moaning.

The crowd parted, to let the horses through. The women threw themselves against the walls.

'Don't come back until you've found her,' cried one.

Pulling on the reins, Ramazan wheeled around; it was Güvercin's mother who had spoken. She was crouching on the ground now, next to Reşit, her head swaying as she slapped her knees and cried.

The muhtar remained inside. Standing back from the window, he watched the crowd grow.

After watching the barber's apprentice run down the street to buy more razor blades, the man in the chair dozed off again. With his face still lathered, he seemed to have turned into a different person: he seemed much calmer now than when he had first sat down.

But the barber still asked, 'Would you like me to wash your face?' The man did not stir. He seemed further and further away, as if he'd been asleep for hours, even days. The barber, meanwhile, took this silence as the man's way of reproaching him for the delay. And so he set down his brush on the edge of the washbasin and turned his eyes to the street.

'I've had enough of this apprentice,' he said. 'He's getting worse every day. He's as stupid as an ape.'

Once again, the man in the chair said nothing. And neither did he move.

Lighting a cigarette, I gazed up at the picture of the dove above the mirror. It seemed out of kilter somehow: it was hard to tell if it had spread its wings to take flight or to land. Its beak seemed angled for sudden flight. Though that could be an illusion, for its eyes, its wings, its breast and even its claws seemed weighed down by fatigue.

To make up for any part I had played in adding to the grim mood, I turned to the barber. 'That picture of a dove – did you do it yourself?'

'I did,' he said, coldly, 'but you've asked me that before.'

'I don't remember that at all,' I said, 'I must have forgotten.'

'You'll doubtless forget again, and ask again, too.'

'Well, as they say, life has a way of repeating itself . . .'

He sat down next to me, and fixed me with his executioner's eyes.

'Oh, yes,' he said, 'life repeats itself. And every repetition is a repetition of something else.'

11

Coming through the door, the muhtar spotted Cıngıl Nuri at the back of the coffeehouse, next to the partridge in its cage. Around him were the usual old men, resting their chins on their canes, or cupping their ears to hear what the others were saying, until falling silent to sink into their thoughts.

As the muhtar settled into the table to Nuri's left, they turned their heads in unison.

'Is it true that Reşit's daughter has been kidnapped?' one asked.

'It's true,' said the muhtar.

He ignored the old men's insinuating smiles. Instead he cradled his tea glass, as its heat passed through his skin. It felt good to say that Güvercin had been kidnapped, actually. It was better than saying she had disappeared. He was afraid of disappearances; they caused such uncertainty. They were so hard to see, or measure, or even grasp. For what had he achieved after Nuri went missing? Nothing! A nothing as great as the nothing he had left behind.

He turned to glance at Nuri. Some sort of shock was passing through him. Trembling, he gulped down his tea. As if to rush back to the past he'd just escaped, almost. As if he hoped to find the path that Güvercin had taken, somewhere inside his own lost years.

Two years he'd been gone, but during that time his children had not stopped growing. In fact, they had grown like cypresses. By now they were almost as tall as Nuri, if not taller. They had, perhaps, added his height to their own, the better to carry him. And that was why there was no way of knowing how often Nuri had wandered the village in his absence, and drunk tea in the coffeehouse or water from the public fountain and conversed with his fellow villagers. As for the child that his wife had claimed to have locked up inside her house – well, that might have been the man himself. Maybe she'd cradled him like the child she'd wished he was – kissed his forehead, even. She had, after all, been so broody of late. The deeper her sons' voices, the hoarser their coughs, and the bolder their stride, the more she had found her husband in them, and that could be another reason why she wrapped her arms so tightly around them, to smother them with kisses. They kept her alive, these kisses. They sated her hunger. They quenched her thirst.

She had, from time to time, read the imam's horoscope; if it promised good tidings, she sank into a gloom. These were times of struggle. She would cry until the fountains of her eyes went dry. For a thousand and one nights, she wrapped her arms around herself and longed to be holding her husband instead. She railed against God for refusing to send him back. Day by day, her resentment grew, to the secret exasperation of the imam. Before long she was singing folk songs to drown out the call to prayer, shouting and screaming the words, or, if her voice failed, banging pots and pans, or throwing those same utensils into the road, even going so far as to roll her eyes and thrust her belly forward like a baby camel, terrorising the children who had gathered around her house.

Following these strange outbursts, rumours spread through the village that God had changed Nuri into a bird, or a lizard, or perhaps even a hunting dog. These rumours grew and grew and the day arrived when, infused with the dust of legend, they unfurled their long tails to sail back to the woman's front door, and strike her dumb. Raising her rheumy eyes to the heavens, she stood for a long time in silence before asking the Lord for forgiveness. Then she asked him again, and again; many hundreds of times, in fact. For hours on end, she went from one courtyard to the next, trying to get God to listen. She even talked to the birds, and the grass on the fields, and the insects, and the frolicking sheep, and the mountains and the blue-eyed babies in their cots. With every passing day she poured more regret into them all, until it had seeped into everything under the sun. But still she was sure she had not done enough. She went to the imam, asking him to guide her in her penance. Falling down on her knees, she burst into tears. The imam listened in silence; then he gazed up at the portrait of the blessed Ali, and the three ropes of prayer beads hanging from a nail, black as dungeons, like a bunch of grapes, and the thyme branches hanging from the rafters. Then, very slowly, he shook his head. Placing his hand on the woman's knee, he quietly cleared his throat, to offer a sweet and musty string of consoling words. The woman paid no attention to his caresses as they climbed from her knees to her hips, and that was why the imam, given courage by her indifference, reached inside her robes, to guide his finger into the most intimate regions of the woman who had come to him seeking guidance. The woman came back again the next day.

This time, her tears flowed even faster. The imam seemed to cry with her. His eyes shone, as dewdrops formed on his eyelashes. Comforted by this sight, the woman cried even harder, until even the adobe walls enclosing them had succumbed to lamentation.

Soon the afternoon prayers had been said. By the time the sun had filtered through the branches of the plum tree to brighten their window, they had made progress. Gently, the imam tossed aside his dungeon-black prayer beads, pulling the woman on to his lap. The room trembled with her sobs – sobs that had begun to sound more forced – as he mumbled another string of comforting words and caressed her breasts. The blessed Ali on the wall closed his eyes. The faster the imam's hands wandered, the louder the woman cried. There followed days of uninterrupted love-making, and uninterrupted crying. She now knew for sure that – even if God had not changed her husband into a lizard, a bird or a hunting dog – he would not be sending him back. Even if he did, he would be turned away, without so much as setting foot in the village, by the imam's call to prayer. If Nuri returned in the guise of a bird, even, he would flap his wings and fly far away . . . Who could know? God might decide to erase him from human memory; he might even send in his creatures one night, to roam the village amidst the chirping insects, sprinkling the powder of forget-fulness over each roof, each street and courtyard . . .

And when they awoke the next morning, not a soul would remember who he was.

When Nuri really did return, no one recognised him.

His greying goatee was caked with dust and soil; his hair matted and wild. He might have been a scarecrow. With every step, he shook off scraps of tin and silver paper. The children tagging behind him raced to see who could pick up the most, sometimes falling to the ground to wrestle with a rival. Nuri's goatee quivered and shook as he walked on, muttering to himself as he went. The children walked alongside him, all the way from the mill to the plane tree, pestering him with questions. Which of them would he make away with? Which of them would he be throwing into his sack? From time to time, Nuri tried to chase them away, or he would whip out a stone and make as if to throw it at them. The first time he did this, the boys took fright, scattering like chicks from a fox. But once they'd worked out he was only pretending, they joined in the game. First they'd pretend to run off, in terror, and then they'd come scrambling back over the courtyard walls to resume the chase. Until, having reached the shade of the plane tree, they were chased off by the men there.

Nuri continued on his way, glancing over his shoulder, to check if anyone was throwing stones. Then he pulled up a chair, to sit with his fellow villagers. It struck them as sorcery, this small change in their routine. Shaken, too, by his contrary manner, they gathered around him, wide-eyed and suspicious. The shoemaker was reminded of the barber, for he, too, had arrived looking worn, wearing rags and the dust of the long road.

The watchman kept a judicious distance, lest his brown uniform give him away. He could not decide if the arrival of this foul-smelling man merited the immediate notification of the muhtar.

They were just about to speak when Nuri, having finished his tea, lit up a cigarette.

Turning to the watchman, he said, 'So, Baki. How are the children doing?'

That took everyone by surprise, of course. The men exchanged wide-eyed glances. The scarecrow guffawed, before falling into a pained silence. As that silence deepened, the villagers exchanged more wide-eyed glances. But they didn't say a word, perhaps just to deepen the torment of curiosity. Finally, he gestured at the barber shop he'd abandoned so many years ago. 'Don't you recognise me?' he cried. 'I'm Nuri. Nuri!'

The villagers froze in their chairs. Stony-faced, they stared at Nuri. No, they thought. It could not be. And then, in a flash, the watchman was running off to find the muhtar. He picked up his rifle and ran through the streets, fast as the wind, and faster than a snake, until at last he came huffing and puffing into the muhtar's courtyard.

Faster now than a bullet from his rifle, or so it seemed to the muhtar as he pushed aside his pan of menemen and rushed off to the village square with his mouth still full. By the time he got there, Nuri was already halfway through his story.

'Tell it from the start,' the muhtar commanded. Pressing down on Nuri's shoulder, he made his suspicions clear.

Asked where he'd been all this time, Nuri said he didn't know. But then, as he sat there, baking in the afternoon sun, he began, very slowly, to explain.

That evening, he'd felt something weighing down on him. At once his skin had felt too tight; his hands no longer fitting his arms, or his feet his legs. His eyes could not see. But he'd known somehow that if only he could open his eyes wide enough, he'd see beyond the cliffs, and perhaps he was already doing so, without knowing it, at that very moment.

Then suddenly his ears grew larger than soup ladles at a wedding. Suddenly he could hear all of them speaking to him. The crate in the corner, the spade handle, the earthenware jug, the broom – they were all talking. Suddenly everything under the sun, without exception, had its own voice. Some groaned, some muttered, some wailed. Some might even have laughed. Nuri, meanwhile, kept looking out of the window. It must be raining, he kept thinking. But he could not see a single drop: and when had it ever rained at this time of the year? This was the voice of the soil, he told himself, as he stood, transfixed, at his window. This was the voice of the trees, the stones, the birds. God in heaven, I can hear the entire world! My ears have been well and truly pierced!

At that point, he had placed his palms on the wall, and the wall had shivered at his touch.

It has a voice. My God, this wall lives, too; it is as alive as all the creatures and plants on this earth . . . He took his hands off the wall, and as darkness descended, the voices now cutting through his ears, his skin and his mind grew ever louder.

While Nuri sat voicelessly on the divan, he was assaulted, from within and without, by the voices of all creation. They were calling on him, these voices. They were telling him to go forth. His eyes passed over each and every object in the house. One by one, his eyes passed over them. He wondered how much they would remember – if he were to leave, what might they retain of his shape, his manner, his voice? Would they remember him at all? If he himself were an object (a candle, for example, or a broom, or tobacco pouch), what of him would remain in the mind of another (say, his wife)? Just the thought was more than he could bear. He left the house, leaving behind a wife cooking spicy tarhana soup, and three children, and his hat.

For hours and hours, he'd walked, but without any hope of leaving. He'd imagined dying – freezing and burning, sated and starving – as he walked away from the village, as far as his legs could take him. It was almost as if the voices inside him were pushing him there. Unless it was something else, a faraway something else, pulling him by the ear. It had surprised him, all this, and at the same time it had sent his spirits soaring. How could it be otherwise? Like it or not, something inside him needed distance. With every step, this something had diminished: drop by drop, it had wasted away. Butterflies had fluttered before his eyes, darkening the world with their tiny, silent wings. All was lost, each was a shiny scale. . . . Each was faceless, each was an eye . . . Each pointed in a different direction . . . Then suddenly there were lights flying towards him, faster than light itself. Hidden behind them were the secrets, the things that had been calling him. As he walked on, lights were lights no longer, but bulls spouting fire. No longer bulls, but camels carrying beaded cradles on their backs. No longer camels but sweaty horses, or herds of goats, or flocks of birds, bearing mirrors aloft. At first the bulls had frightened him and sent him scurrying for cover in a field of thorns. But then, when he'd gone after the birds – the birds bearing mirrors aloft – his heart had begun to beat with theirs. Only to see that the bulls were actually horses. That was when he'd decided to turn back. Even so, he was still glad to have attempted escape. Even though it had weakened his legs somewhat. It had sometimes seemed to him that he'd grown forelegs, and more legs, just in front of them, and in front of those, even more . . .

And it had seemed as if, beyond these legs, there were yet more legs, invisibly pushing him along. Behind all these, there was the faint spectre he left behind. Unless he was imagining himself in front of himself, and beyond that, and at the same time, behind it . . .

Nuri paused to take a breath. He could have carried on with those horses. He could have mounted them there and then, to gallop off into the mountains, never to be seen again . . . But a hand had held him back. Whose hand it was, he could not say. And neither could he say whose mind controlled it. It would be years before he was at last able to solve the mystery of this hand: it was his own. But it was caught between two other hands. If they were in fact hands: at the time he wasn't even sure of that.

He'd not ridden off with the horses, of course. Instead, he'd continued on foot. The village was far behind him by now. Looking over his shoulder, he could no longer see its candles flickering. The soil under his feet was slipping away fast, very fast. So fast, in fact, that he'd found himself back on the plain – though what plain that was, he couldn't say. All he could say was that the silence there was as deep as the darkness. There he had sat, listening to the drumbeat of his heart. That was when he had seen a shooting star. When it had vanished, to parts unknown, Nuri had stood up again, and off he had gone, padding into the heart of the night. Later still, he had grasped the truth of the matter; he was neither walking nor standing still. He had been walking on the spot, and standing still while walking. As in a dream, almost . . . However fast he ran, he would never arrive; the longer he walked, the greater his hope of arriving.

There, before him, were the shining lights. Then, overcome by desire, his arms stretched as far as they could go . . . To be left with nothing. The nothing that turned thoughts into dreams . . . Step by step, Nuri had lost himself in darkness; the light that had promised him horses, camels, birds and mirrors was still far off. Now he was surrounded by creatures he could not see. But he could hear them panting as they paced around him without rest, jingling their bells as they went. It was almost as if they were trying to break him – force his surrender – release them to burrow into his eyes, feet and hands. At this point, Nuri had felt himself surrounded by rustling of fabrics, and the beating of drums and moans of uncertain meaning. But the moment Nuri had stopped walking, those sounds stopped, too. And then, when Nuri resumed his journey, the cries of joy returned, until, with a great yawn, he'd swallowed them all. Perhaps he'd died, Nuri thought, and was among the musicians of hell. Who could know where this journey had taken him? Who could know what traces it would leave in his memory? Would his arms thicken like handles of a sharp-edged spade, or was this body of his destined to become nothing more than a ripple in the soil, and in the history of the village? He could not – could never – know. Just as he could never know what had pulled him back. He recalled a yellow sea, as bright as it was dark, a red sea, as red as blood, a joyless sea, bereft of laughter, bobbing with houses, and rubbish, and oil, and the stinking skeletons of humankind and fish . . . Together they had crossed that sea, but how many years had it taken and by what means had they achieved this feat?

Then, in a patch of shade, in the middle of the desert, they had met a barber. With him were two men waiting to be shaved. One was fingering his prayer beads, which were as black as dungeons. The man next to him was short and frail, and not quite there. Indeed, the second man seemed almost not to exist and perhaps he actually didn't. He could have been an empty space and nothing more, an empty space occupying the chair next to the man with the prayer beads, and shaped like a man. So what Nuri had done next was to occupy that space. And there he'd sat, in silence, under the barber's gaze . . . And soon that empty space (though shaped by another) had come to feel like his own.

But then another man – a tall man – had come striding into his patch of shade. The barber had raised his scissors high in the air, as if to stab it. 'Welcome, my good sir,' he greeted him. Then, five minutes later, he asked, 'Are you still writing a novel?' 'I am,' the man had said. He'd then fallen silent, to stare at the picture of the dove above the mirror. And who could have thought it? The longer this man kept his eyes on that picture, the more Nuri's goatee had grown. And this might be why the barber had passed over the man with the dungeon beads, and called Nuri to the chair first. At once, Nuri had settled himself inside the mirror. For days on end, the barber had gone on clicking his scissors, as he and his apprentice danced around Nuri's chair. And then, a drum had sounded in the distance; rustling fabric had piled up under his feet. How hot it was suddenly. How very hot! They'd come closer to the sun, no doubt – there were no birds in this sky, which was no longer blue. It was almost as if the very idea of blue was a rare memory, held only in the minds of those who still dared to look up at the firmament, as all creation went plunging into blackest night.

God only knew what the time was, but finally the barber had tired. Because as fast as he cut Nuri's hair, it kept growing back. He, too, had tired of the barber's endless clipping. Seeing no point in staying, he had jumped to his feet and left.

Emerging from the mirror, he had found himself back in the sea again: that same yellow sea. It could have been the desert, dreaming of a sea, or the sea, dreaming of a desert – there was no knowing, either way. He was walking, of course. Walking towards the blinking lights – towards that mirror, held aloft by the birds – for those lights still called out to him. The waters now came up to his chin – came up to his chin in waves – and there were people, standing at the windows of their sea shacks. Silence had wiped their mouths from their faces, which were far away and dark as night, and shaped like eyes. Nuri, meanwhile, was left to make his way through the waves – they were red as blood and he didn't even know how to swim. With all his strength, he fought the urge to swallow the whole sea. Then suddenly night had fallen; and with it had come a shower of silver, moonlit sparks . . .

He could smell the blood in the sea now, just as he could chart its calm depths. It seemed to him now that everything under the sun was in the sea with him: the trees, the mountains, the grasslands, and all the sky's stars . . . And Nuri. He was in the water, too. And he was tired. He let himself drift, as the water grew ever thicker. It had, in his sleep, taken on the consistency of gum. It was the deep and deathly sleep of legends.

Nuri could not recall what time he had woken up – only that he had opened his eyes to find himself inside a great marble mansion. The lights on the ceiling sparkled like rainbows, and lining the walls were lamps, and candles. But they kept licking up at each other; they served not to spread light but to conjure up an illusion. The memory of a lost era, perhaps, or a future not yet released from the past. Nuri, meanwhile, was dancing in their midst, shaking the bells on his fingers . . . He was alone in this mansion, but once again he could hear fabric rustling and invisible creatures breathing. Nuri knew they were watching him dance, because every once in a while, when he shook his bells, they would applaud.

Then Nuri began to wonder how he was able to dance for so long without stopping; especially as he didn't know how to dance. Even at his own wedding, under the tired, pleading eyes of the zurna player, he had only just managed a few claps of the hand. He thought then that those invisible creatures might know nothing of dance. Perhaps they thought he was dancing every time he moved.

Then suddenly it was all clear to him. Suddenly it all made sense. He wasn't dancing, he was winnowing. He was reaping the harvest with his scythe, or riding a donkey, cutting firewood, sitting on the soil watching the sun . . . At that same moment, he remembered the village. 'This means,' he said, 'that everything I have lived through has been a dance. It means that whatever a man does is a part of a dance . . . It means that I was dancing in the village; when I beat my children, made love to my wife, killed an ailing sheep, gathered fruit, brought children into the world, buried my dead, ploughed the soil, watched a bird, shaved the villagers or said hello, voted for the muhtar, sat in the coffeehouse . . .'

The day broke and the lights in the great marble mansion switched off one by one until nothing remained apart from the flickering candles, dying oil lamps, and Nuri's jingling bells . . . At that moment, he was struck by a thought . . . 'If I stop,' he said, 'if I shake these bells one last time, and stop, what would happen? Would I begin to see my invisible spectators? Would I suddenly see everything? What would

I become? Would I die?' When a thought strikes a man, he is already halfway down the road to a new place; he is, at least, no longer where he was, and there is no turning back. For those who turn back leave a part of themselves behind. Nuri tore the bells off his fingers, tossing them away like clipped fingernails. Rushing to the window, he was met by the scorching sun. Then, the houses . . . The streets were clogged with human and animal skeletons; the houses with spiders' webs. On the rooftops were blanched bird bones, their dust scattered by the wind. The streets were deserted; nothing drew breath. The stink was appalling. It rose in waves of heat, like smoke.

Nuri went outside. He wandered a while among the piles of shredded plastic bags and the floods of prayer beads. Goats' hooves attached themselves to his feet, then rabbit tails, fezzes and cat skeletons. How long he had searched for succour in that fearsome valley of death, how far he had travelled across that ocean of stinking rubbish, Nuri could not say. He just kept walking . . . He kept walking because he could still see that mirror, held aloft by those birds. He was sure that when he reached them, he would find himself at last – and save himself. The birds, meanwhile, kept flapping their wings. They kept flying. Far away they flew, as a thousand and one visions sparkled in the mirror. They could already see where they were going, these birds. They were already there, in the mirror they held aloft . . .

Later, Nuri saw himself on a vast plain. Then suddenly he was entering a forest; a green colossus seemed to grow before his eyes. He could hear snakes hissing as they slid between the pines: there was a strange rustling, and stirrings that the eye couldn't catch. Where to go? How to escape the green incubus? Just then, at the point where the darkness swallowed up the pines, he saw a man. A man who was tired and spent. He carried a sack on his back. His nose was moist from grumbling. He kept his eyes on the ground, and the lower his face fell, the more it looked as if it would fall away altogether, to strip his real face bare.

'Your tea's gone cold, muhtar,' said Nuri.

The muhtar startled. He swung to look at Nuri, who was sitting on his right. Nuri was holding his head in his hands, and giggling.

Unable to fathom why this man could be giggling, the muhtar fixed him with a fierce stare. Then he gave up, to stare at the desk before him. And once again, he got a shock.

There was no tea.

12

Although much time had passed, the apprentice had still not returned with the razor blades. The man in the chair had begun to lose patience. Every two seconds, he turned his soapy face to glare at the road. But aside from honking vehicles of various colours, there was nothing to see. For reasons unknown, the crowds thronging the streets had thinned and thinned, until they'd vanished altogether.

'In the old days, you never put blades into a razor,' said the man in the chair. 'You'd sharpen steel instead.'

The barber said nothing. He was sitting in the next chair like a new customer, waiting his turn. From time to time, he'd glance into the mirror. He was exceedingly calm; he seemed even to have forgotten that his apprentice had gone off to buy razor blades. Had I asked, he'd most certainly claim to have no memory of it.

'Or else,' continued the man in the chair, 'there'd be a belt at the corner of the counter and the razors would be sharpened on that . . .'

The barber stayed silent. So silent, in fact, that the man in the chair decided to do the same. He kept looking out at the road, and each time he did, he heaved a sigh. Then a weight fell over him. Leaning back in his chair, he began, very slowly, to click his dungeon beads, one by one. But this didn't last. The space between the clicks grew longer, and then longer still, until, at last, there was no clicking at all.

My eyes met the barber's. At that moment, it seemed to me that we were both thinking the same thing.

'Is he asleep?' I whispered.

'I think he is,' said the barber, 'but not here.'

13

Musa Dede had his wooden leg stretched out like a plank from an old ox-cart: he was sitting in a dark alcove, with his beard in his lap. The muhtar waited outside, next to the sheaves of corn, until he could hear the sage's voice. Then he entered his shadowy domain, feeling his way past the sacks of wheat, as Musa Dede watched.

'Have you heard?' asked the muhtar.

'Yes,' said Musa Dede, 'I have. Güvercin's gone missing.'

Placing his hands on his knees, the muhtar stared into Musa Dede's cavernous eyes.

'I came for your wise counsel,' he said in a faltering voice.

'From a blind man in his nineties?'

'Yes.'

'So you're that desperate, are you?'

The muhtar opened his arms.

'Yes,' he said, 'I'm desperate, desperately desperate.'

Musa Dede muttered something to himself, something unintelligible. He kept stroking his beard, as if it had somehow absorbed the muhtar's desperation.

'So. What do you think happened to Güvercin the Dove?'

'I have no idea,' said the muhtar. 'She either went off of her own accord, or she was kidnapped. I've sent Mustafa and Ramazan off to the neighbouring villages to make enquiries.'

Musa Dede smiled. It bothered the muhtar, this smile. He couldn't begin to read it.

'Have you ever heard of Fatma of the Mirrors?'

'I know the name,' replied the muhtar. 'I heard her mentioned when I was just a boy.'

Musa Dede fell silent, as his face grew steadily darker.

'Fatma of the Mirrors,' he murmured at long last, in a faraway voice, 'Fatma of the Mirrors is a bird. It could well be that Güvercin is herself now inside that selfsame mirror.'

The muhtar was at a loss for words. He stared at Musa Dede, trying to decide whether or not the man had gone senile. But he could not.

'Fatma of the Mirrors is a bird,' Musa Dede said once again. 'I don't know her either . . . I've never set eyes on her. Even so, I can still see her eyes. Dark as molasses they are. Round as two cups. Because she left behind her eyes, you know. And she left them behind a cabin. They must have torn it down by now. It was just below the cliffs. No one ever went in there. No one could have. Was it cursed, or was it sacred? I have no idea. It may well have been both . . . Because, as rumour had it, Fatma of the Mirrors was both whore and saint. During the War of Independence, whole battalions of soldiers on the run found solace between her legs. Some had fled the army; others were heading back; others still were on their way to joining the brigands; whatever took them up into the mountains on a cold evening, they warmed their hands on her breasts. She was their mother, their wife, their sister, and their confidante. Because she fled with the deserters, and accompanied the captured, died with the dying . . . She even had a legendary tryst with the golden-toothed Soldier Hamdi . . . Soldier Hamdi, who could do alone what an entire company might struggle to achieve . . . To make him a pair of sandals, you'd need an entire ox-skin, if not more. If he went to a wedding, the cooks would despair . . . Because Soldier Hamdi could devour entire mountains of pilaf with his two hands, and bolt down stewed fruit by the cupful. He'd walk down the street clutching his stomach as if it were a big fat drum . . . But as it happened, Fatma's feminine charms were more talked about than Hamdi's girth. If they spoke of Hamdi once, they spoke of Fatma a hundred times over. So it turned into a bit of a competition; knowingly or not, people were goading them on. And soon they were homing in on each other: now and again, here and there, they would let it be known that one of these days, there'd be a showdown. And finally, that day arrived. It might have been on a deserted street, and it might have been in a crowd, but the two came face to face. Fatma of the Mirrors throws him a skittish glance. Soldier Hamdi twirls his moustache and smiles, but behind that smile is a silken dagger . . . Then suddenly – and who is to know who took whom – they end up shut away in that cabin. Meanwhile, the village waits, and waits, in anxious anticipation. What goes on inside will forever remain a secret. They could be fighting or they could be making love. From time to time, they can be heard screaming, pleading, laughing. But still no one dares approach the door of that house. Because the man they call Soldier Hamdi is trouble made flesh; he could break every bone in a man's body. And then what? Either you curled up in a corner and died, or you went from door to door, begging for a crumb of bread. Then one day, they saw Fatma in the orchard, covered in sweat. Her buttocks wobbled as she limped. And that was the last time anyone saw Fatma. There were those who said that she had retired to a migrants' village, to live as a penitent, rising from her prayer rug only to retrieve her prayer beads. Others said that she was carried off by angels, on account of her fine service to the nation during the War of Independence. Perhaps she was up there with the Lord, reclining on a green divan . . . Wherever she went, the fact was she had given comfort to many dozens of soldiers who had gone back to the front to fight with even greater ardour, filled as they were with memories of the warmth and beauty of the nation they had left behind. And also, the shepherds found Soldier Hamdi in the cabin. He was lying on his cloak. Still wearing his army boots. His face still locked in the moment of triumph . . . They loaded him on their backs and returned him to the village. They laid out his stiff body before his nine wives and their army of children. And then two soldiers swooped in from somewhere. They asked the villagers to tell them where Hamdi was. Don't hide him from us, they said. Meanwhile, Hamdi was laid out in that courtyard: dead. Well, he might be dead, but he was still a deserter. The muhtar of the day got a horse-cart ready for the soldiers, and off they went with Hamdi, in that cart pulled by two horses that whinnied just as skittishly as Fatma . . . A few months passed, and a letter arrived, announcing that Hamdi had been killed at the front. Everyone was shocked, of course. Everyone became very confused about Hamdi. And I myself am confused to this day. If Hamdi is the Hamdi who died at the front, then who was the Hamdi who succumbed to Fatma's fatal charms? . . . Or was that Hamdi no more than a reflection caught in Fatma's mirror – a reflection, no less, of Hamdi at the front? And where did Fatma go, where did she spend the rest of her life, where did she die? My friend, I cannot for the life of me answer these questions . . . Not even after all these years. And now, if you like, I can ask you another question. This Hamdi had a courtyard full of children, born of his nine wives . . . Where are they now? I wonder. Who are they? What do you think?'

The muhtar rose slowly. And then he left, leaving Musa Dede's question unanswered. When he reached the courtyard, he was shaking, and muttering, 'Damnation! Damnation!'

14

The muhtar's wife looked up when she heard his footsteps.

'Is it you?' she asked, while making it clear she had no need for an answer. 'You look like you've come back from the dead,' she added. 'Is there no news of Güvercin?'

At that moment the courtyard gate creaked. They turned to look. It was the watchman. Panting heavily, he ran up to the muhtar.

'What's the news?' asked the muhtar.

'We've had a sighting!'

'Do you mean to say you've found Güvercin?' the woman asked.

'You stay out of this,' said the muhtar. 'Go back inside.'

He walked to the gate and the watchman followed.

'Where?'

'At home, sitting by the window.'

'And you've been keeping watch, I take it? Any activity?'

'Nothing at all. Unless you count sitting.'

'Even people who spend the whole day sitting do things. You must have seen something.'

'Well, yes. I saw a pile of paper.'

'What sort of paper?'

The watchman stretched out his arm. He was trying to give some sense of what he'd seen, but he got confused, wondering how exactly to describe paper, so he ended up tracing a strange shape in the air.

'Paper,' he said, swallowing.

'Don't forget to make a note of that,' the muhtar said. 'Store it away, somewhere in that head of yours!'

The watchman nodded.

As they walked back to the village square, the light began to fade. From the cliffs came the sound of bells; as they stood at their courtyard gates, waiting for their herds to come home, the women of the village chattered amongst themselves. The muhtar and the watchman fell silent, without quite knowing why. Forgetting each other, they gazed up at the cliffs. The muhtar stepped into his office, looking perplexed.

'Did you see what I saw?' he asked in a whisper.

'I don't think I did,' the watchman replied.

'We just walked through the village, but not a single person acknowledged our presence!'

The watchman didn't know what to say. Mystified by the muhtar's words, he concentrated instead on the village square. Flocks of sheep were flowing in from all sides, kicking up clouds of dust and smoke. A few squealing children were running after the sheep, and trying to mount them.

'Did you ever meet Soldier Hamdi?' asked the muhtar.

'I've heard of him.'

'What was he known for?'

'A handlebar moustache.'

The muhtar smiled. He wasn't in the mood to smile, but he couldn't help himself. The absurd thought crossed his mind that the watchman's answers had been scripted many years ago.

'So that's what you say he was known for? A handlebar moustache?'

The watchman nodded. Still smiling, the muhtar gave him a long hard look. The man had no moustache of any kind.

'All right, then,' he said. 'Let me ask you something else. If Hamdi the Soldier really did take nine women to bed every night of his life, then it would not be unreasonable to assume that this scoundrel with the handlebar moustache left behind a few children. Haven't you ever wondered who they are?'

The watchman's mouth fell open. It had never occurred to him to wonder about Soldier Hamdi's children. For a time he didn't move. Then he turned towards the houses fast melting into the darkness, studying each door and window in turn.

'They're here,' said the muhtar.

They arrived on two horses. Against the dark night, their racing forms fluttered like white butterflies. They were galloping into the wind. The closer they came, the more distant the echo of their hammering hooves. Caught between the approaching image and the receding thunder, the two spectral horses seemed to be galloping on the spot. Hours later, they stopped outside the muhtar's office.

'Speak,' said the muhtar.

'We've looked everywhere,' said the two shadows, but they stayed on their horses.

'And?'

'No one's seen or heard from her.'

The muhtar dismissed them with a peremptory wave of the hand. The horses wheeled around, giving off the scent of hot sweat, and soon they were lost to the darkness and the distant lamplight. The muhtar was left wondering how they could have returned with this news, only to gallop off again. 'It's like a dream,' he told himself, 'it's as if they were never here. Perhaps they never were. Perhaps I imagined them, or saw them in a dream. Only one thing is certain. That wasn't Ramazan and Mustafa we just saw . . .'

The watchman was still standing there, staring into the darkness. When he spoke, he took the muhtar by surprise. 'Güvercin is lost, too,' he said with a heavy sigh, 'like Hamdi's children . . .'

'Shut your mouth,' murmured the muhtar, 'don't tell me she's lost! And we don't even know if Hamdi had any!'

They fell quiet for a moment. The watchman was losing his bearings.

'Maybe you're not even here!' said the muhtar. He was losing his temper.

The watchman was even more confused now. He touched his rifle with his right palm; it was cold. He took a deep breath. He tried to summon the strength to question his own existence, but this seemed too silly, and he could not help but smile. The muhtar was not amused.

'Don't imagine I'm going to let you smirk at me,' he snapped. 'Anyone would think you were pleased she's vanished! Go and keep watch on Cennet's son! See if he's sneaking out after dark, and if he does, find out where he's going.'

The watchman walked away.

A few hours later, he was hiding in the dark, watching Cennet's son. He had his eyes closed, but only to slow down his breathing. Once he had done so he went back to watching Cennet's son, who was in one of the upstairs rooms. He had set his lamp close to the window, no doubt, and the shadows it cast on to the inner wall were hard to read. Every once in a while the flame flared up to send shadows racing across the ceiling. Now and again the flame would go out, just like that, and then there would be a long stretch when the wall went as blank as a mirror made of earth. But then Cennet's son came back again, carrying a sheaf of paper. He sat down on the windowsill and began to write. On and on he wrote, as the night grew ever darker. Every so often, he raised his eyes to stare into the darkness. No doubt he could see the watchman hiding under the eaves, pressed against the house and sneaking a cigarette.

The watchman shifted his weight. His nerves were getting to him. He didn't like people watching him when he was meant to be the one watching them. Whether he thought about it or not, he was tired. He leant his rifle against the wall and let himself slide slowly to the ground. By now the village had sunk into a silence so deep that there was hardly any village left. As if it had been too long in this world, and exhausted all its resources. As he pondered this thought, he felt himself falling into a bottomless pit. This must be the end, he decided. He was taking his leave from the world he knew, and never coming back. He had no hands. No feet, no nose. Were it not for that light breeze on his face, he'd have no skin either. Maybe he was flying. Maybe one day he'd fall back to earth, to find peace and quiet, and a place to sleep. How long would it be before he opened his eyes? What was this great marble mansion he saw standing before him? Why was his finger on the bell? Loud whispers crowded in on him. Faint, humming and dark, like a line of ants feeding on Cıngıl Nuri. Was there anyone here he didn't know? First came the muhtar. On his right was Ramazan; on his left, Mustafa. But Ramazan wasn't Ramazan. More likely he was Ferit the bandit. Mustafa, who wasn't Mustafa, must be Soldier Hamdi with Fatma in his sights. A vineyard crumbled at the sight of her. A soldier – a tired, fearful deserter with a rifle in his hand. He was here, too. But where was the yard holding the children Hamdi had sired with his nine women?

'What news?'

The watchman jumped. Where had the muhtar come from?

'No news,' he said.

'And Cennet's son?'

'He's still inside.'

The muhtar nodded. Then he walked straight to the front door of Cennet's son's house. The watchman was surprised at this sudden move. He found himself wondering whether or not it was the real muhtar. None of this made any sense – it must be a dream he was watching, a fit of delirium, an unearthly dance. Now he couldn't even decide how to hold his rifle. First he tried slinging it from his shoulder; then he tried holding it in his hands. When he caught up with the muhtar, he felt as if he had dragged the night to the door with him. He could almost feel it sliding across all the rooftops of the village. He and the muhtar were wedged now between the door and the darkened village. But they had come too far now to think of turning around.

So it was with some reluctance that the muhtar knocked on the door. The knock ripped through the air like a clap of thunder. The whole village must be awake now. The watchman could feel their eyes pressing against the night. He thought about the village elders, shivering on their mattresses, and the children, jumping out of bed, and the animals kicking in their stables, ready to bolt. As an old lamp cast Cennet's shadow across the walls, the watchman began to shake.

'Who is it?'

'It's me, open up!'

Slowly the door swung open. Cennet stood on the doorstep, her headscarf half undone, hair flying everywhere.

'What is it?'

The muhtar said nothing. Instead he looked down at Cennet's bare feet.

'Where's the girl?'

'Who?'

'The girl!'

Cennet's eyes settled on the rifle, which was shining in the darkness. Losing patience, the muhtar pushed past the old woman into the house. The watchman followed. Together they ran up the unlit stairs. Cennet's son was waiting for them at the door.

'Where's Güvercin?' cried the muhtar.

The younger man looked at him as though he were mad.

'Tell me, where have you taken her?'

'I've not kidnapped anyone.'

The muhtar went hurtling into the room, going straight for the papers on the divan. He rifled through them, pausing now and again to hold a sheet up to the lamplight for a closer look.

'What are these?' he asked, after a pause.

'Letters,' said Cennet's son.

The muhtar began pacing the room like a sleepwalker, papers in hand. It was as if he hadn't heard.

The watchman was harder to read. He wasn't following the muhtar's footsteps, but he wasn't staying still either. With strange little half-steps, he was tracing a path around the house. It was almost as if he was circling an object only he could see. Cennet's son seemed unmoved as he watched the strange proceedings. He leant against the doorframe, as calm as an actor waiting for his cue.

The muhtar had moved on to the next room now. He was peering into the humid darkness, checking behind the piled sacks of chickpeas, and underneath the staircase, going into the pantry to examine each and every shelf.

'Take him to my office,' he told the watchman.

Prodded by the butt of the watchman's rifle, Cennet's son made no protest. His mother watched trembling from the top of the stairs. Her headscarf was in her hand, and at that moment, with her dress and her fluttering hair, she looked more like an angel than like herself. Perhaps this was why she had lost the power of speech: she was moving her lips, but soundlessly.

'Look at me,' the muhtar ordered when they met her at the top of the stairs. 'If you know anything about this, I'm asking you to tell us now, because otherwise this morning will start very late. And let me warn you: there's no remedy on this earth for time wasted.'

'What would I know?' she asked.

'You know something. Think about it. If you don't know, you must have suspected something. You're his mother.'

'No,' said Cennet, 'I know nothing, and I suspect nothing either. Let go of my son!' The muhtar continued down the stairs. Cennet set her lamp on the ground and sat on the top step, looking down at them.

'Desperation has made your eyes blind,' she said.

Still shaking, she walked out to the porch. She tried to make out the village square in the dark. She looked from house to house, street to street. She wanted to see every part of it and touch it – no, caress it. She could see nothing but the pitch-black night. Stretching out her arms she stepped forward.

'Perhaps,' she thought, 'it is the village which is still here, while I have been left somewhere else.'

15

The barber was staring at the man in the chair.

'Who can say how many times he's dozed off now,' he said in a soft whisper.

I offered no reply. Every time this man fell asleep, the silence in the shop deepened. Everything – from the scissors to the razors, from the boxes of powder to the bottles of cologne, from the brushes to the towels, and the walls, and even the water-heater – seemed fogged with sleep.

'Maybe he's dreaming,' said the barber.

There followed a short silence. Who was to know which one of us started this – but something had grasped us, and the entire shop, in the palms of its hands. I was struggling for breath now. I gave my fellow prisoner a sidelong glance.

'Maybe he's dreaming,' the barber said.

I was not quite sure if he said this twice; it felt as if time had somehow divided us.

Nevertheless I said, 'Yes. Maybe he's dreaming. But will he remember any of it, when he wakes up?'

16

The watchman jumped up when the door opened, but Cennet's son remained seated in his chair next to the wall, indifferent to the anger in the room.

'Get up, boy!' roared the watchman.

As soon as Cennet's son got up, the muhtar sat down. He made himself comfortable. He imagined waves of silence, rolling across the room, swamping the young man across from him, and lapping against his heart. The letters were there on the desk, right next to his elbow. Each and every one was a piece of evidence. He still had no idea what they proved, but as soon as he read them, all would be clear.

Without thinking, he lit a cigarette. With the first drag, he went into a coughing fit. First, he cursed himself for breaking the silence he'd nurtured with such care. And for what? Or maybe it was just as well, he thought: maybe he'd needed to cough, to make it clear that this silence was his creation and his alone. But then he saw that both the watchman and Cennet's son were watching him cough. He waited for one of them to say something. When no one did, he again lost his patience. But it was small and indistinct, the ill-will he felt then. As long as it didn't engulf them all, it could be forgiven.

While the muhtar sat there at his desk like a statue of a god, the watchman underwent a transformation. Soon he had turned into a watchman who knew no mercy. He was standing behind Cennet's son, breathing down his neck. With every passing moment his body grew harder. And who could say? He might have been standing in that spot for many thousands of years, in different uniforms, with different muhtars and under different names, but now he was the man of that moment, turned to stone.

Finally, the muhtar turned to Cennet's son.

In a voice of authority, he said, 'Tell us what you did with the girl?'

'Are you out of your mind?' cried Cennet's son. 'I have nothing to do with her!'

The muhtar gave the boy an insinuating smile – or rather, he thought of smiling as he struggled to hide the overwhelming urge to throw the young man against the wall . . . However, the muhtar's face didn't actually move, remaining as sullen and impassive as before. The moment he became aware of this, he beckoned Cennet's son to his side. As he shunted the letters across his desk, he asked, 'What are these?'

'Letters.'

'I know that. Who are they for?'

'No one!'

The muhtar's face went red. He put his trembling hands into his waistcoat pockets and pulled them out again. He looked to either side. What was he to do? Frowning, he shook his head, picked up one of the letters, and began to read it out. When he was done, he read out another, and then another . . . The margins were adorned with flowers whose stems unfurled into the corners, like snakes. At the end of some of the letters were sketches of birds holding envelopes in their beaks. With each new appearance, the birds changed their direction of flight, as if to mirror each other. But the muhtar hadn't yet noticed that they were reversed. He was too intent on deciphering the scrawled words. They contained pages about love ('such a burden it would take two to carry it') and the rhythm of love, and the beloved's breasts, and the lover's long walks among the wildflowers, accepting his own death, so long as death came to him sooner than it came to her, for this was how it came to pass that lovers could die, from the burden of love itself.

But nowhere in these missives of love, sadness and longing did he mention the girl by name.

The muhtar was beside himself. 'Did you write these?'

'I did,' said Cennet's son.

'Like hell you did!' bellowed the muhtar. 'You haven't got the brains to string together two words. Tell me, then. Who were you writing to?'

'No one!'

The muhtar pushed aside the letters in disgust. Rising from his chair, he walked to the window. As if he wanted to escape, almost. As if he had nothing left to say. From here on in, he was going to keep his distance, seeing nothing, touching less. He peered between the curtains. 'So he wrote these letters to no one,' he thought, looking into the darkness. 'No one . . .' He tried to conjure up that murky shadow, that entity he'd never met or seen. But no matter how hard he stared into nothingness, no face emerged.

'Look here,' he said, turning around, 'I know what it's like to be young . . . I didn't emerge bearded from the womb, you know? No matter how they steel their hearts, the young fall in love. Maybe you've fallen in love: I'm not saying you shouldn't have – quite the contrary – I'm just saying you should go about it properly! Don't smear your face in it like mud, or your name, either! How many times did you send your shitty-knickered mother to Reşit to ask for his daughter's hand without anything to show for it? Did you even send her once? Let's say you didn't. Let's say some ruffian took you into a corner and whispered some infidel words into your ear and you grabbed the girl and kidnapped her. This is youth we're talking about, anything can happen! But what's done is done, the dead are dead . . . Tell me where the girl is, and then we can talk to her father and bring this matter to a satisfactory conclusion. Where's the girl?'

But still Cennet's son kept quiet. So quiet, in fact, that his silence leaked out of the walls of the muhtar's office, swallowing every sound in its path as it rolled towards the village square. The muhtar leant back against the wall and looked at his outstretched hands; they no longer seemed to belong to him. There were living, breathing creatures, with fears and secrets they would never share with him.

What happened next was beyond comprehension. That said – by the time the muhtar began lowing like a calf, they had all lost their way. First the candle had flickered. Then it had died. It was still dark, and in that darkness were fists clenched with rage. And kicks, and shouts, and long strings of curses. The watchman's cap flew off his head, only to be caught again and then lost again, and crushed. By now Cennet's son was sobbing violently, and trying to crawl away. Then he, too, was flying through the air like the cap. He, too, was crushed. No one could say how long the fray lasted. But when, with trembling hands, the watchman relit the candle, Cennet's son was on the floor, writhing in pain. The blows had painted his temples with blood. He struggled to open his eyes. He looked at the watchman, and then swallowed a few times, as if he hoped that this would be the end of it. Averting his eyes, the watchman righted the overturned chairs. In a room so small, this was no mean feat: wherever he looked he met that bloodied face, with those half-dead eyes staring up at him. And perhaps that was why he kept moving around the chairs, until he gave up and lined them against the wall. Then he searched for his cap. Once he had solved this small mystery, he began to calm down. It didn't take him long to spot it; the cap was lying underneath Cennet's son. But how to retrieve it – that was another question. In the end he just sat there, letting his mind wander, and scratching his head.

The muhtar had had enough. Resting his head in his hands, he wondered about the nobody that Cennet's son had created out of nothing. He could just not believe that all those letters were written to someone with no name, and perhaps even no body. No one in the village had the brains for that, quite simply. Unless you included Soldier Hamdi, and his courtyard full of children, and Fatma of the Mirrors, and the pedlar who came and went like a ghost, and Güvercin the Dove . . . And now there were these letters, written to no one. Out of nothing. Another nothing! A nothing with no name, no face, no soul!

The muhtar leant back; gazing down at the pools of blood on the floor, he asked himself if there was a pool of nothingness inside each and every one of them. He instantly regretted not having thought of this long ago. Could he be right? If each and every one of them had a nobody inside them, then the whole village was full of nobodies who came and went like ordinary people, stopping at the coffeehouse, working the fields, gathering in the shade of the plane tree, crying at funerals and dancing at weddings. The muhtar knew nothing of these nobodies: he'd never met a single one. And this could be because the villagers had kept their nobodies well hidden. Perhaps each and every one of them had been nurturing their own nobodies in secret. Each, perhaps, in his own way. Some had fed their nobodies with dreams, night after night. Some had given them lullabies to drink. Some had nourished them with folk songs and legends. Some had put them to sleep with their voices, or caressed them with silence. Some fed their nobodies from their own flesh, and clothed them with their own skins. Cennet's son had fed his nobody with letters; he had caressed his secret nobody with words. With the flowers he had drawn in the margins, he had created its scent. With the birds, he had created his nobody's voice. Its eyebrows, its tresses, its lips, its eyes; they were all made of letters. He may even, invisibly, have fashioned its movements, so that this nameless nobody might wander from room to room without his mother ever noticing, climbing stairs made from letters, sitting at the dining table, cooking soup with Cennet, passing her the salt, and drinking water, but never, ever taking its eyes off Cennet, because if this nobody was not Cennet herself, then it was one of her dreams. Which meant, perhaps, that Cennet had come to inhabit another life, thinking it a dream, when really she was living the life of a nobody . . .

'Poor old Cennet,' he mumbled.

That made Cennet's son sit up.

As the midnight inquisition resumed, shadows began to gather again outside the muhtar's office. All evening, they had been coming and going, creeping out of their courtyards to watch. As if by common agreement, no one spoke. And yet there were whispers, rising from some unknown quarter to float through the dark streets; growing in volume, they rose above the chimneys, trees and walls to flow towards the village square. At first glance, each shadow seemed to stand alone, but then the truth emerged: they were as one, reflecting each other like broken mirrors, scattering their fears across every stone, patch of earth or darkness. They grew and grew like secrets. They had long since outgrown their owners, whom they had left behind at home to fret with their wives and children, but with every step they took, they took another step on their owners' behalf. And now they were standing in silence outside the muhtar's office, watching his door as yet more shadows poured out from behind the plane tree. Then these shadows, too, sat down, adding themselves to the silent crowd. If just one of them had shed a tear, the others would have followed. If just one had stood up, they would all have walked together . . . But they couldn't make up their minds; they didn't know what to do about the shouting and banging and cursing coming out of the muhtar's office. Pressed down by silence, their anxieties grew. And they grew too, filling up the village square, turning it black as tar. And there they stood, waiting: the night within the night.

By now the muhtar's anger was all but spent. He was still kicking and punching Cennet's son, but with one ear on the door. He thought he could hear people breathing outside. 'The band of nobodies,' he said to himself. 'They've arrived!' At that same moment, all sound ceased. So great was the silence that the muhtar had to ask himself if there was a new sort of nothingness out there, wandering amongst the nobodies.

The muhtar froze . . . Casting the watchman a side-long glance, he directed his attention to the door. At that same moment, they heard, or seemed to hear, what sounded like hundreds of hands, all swaying together, then hundreds of fingernails scratching the door. The watchman caught his breath, but the muhtar managed to convince himself that this must be an illusion. He lit a cigarette. Took a deep drag. Armed in smoke, he strode fearlessly across the room.

He threw open the door, flooding the village square with candlelight. Before him was a sea of faces, and hats, and shoulders and hands: a great mute mass, shuddering with the night; a vast expanse of flashing eyes that gave the muhtar pause. But this was the moment to stand up to them. Let them stare, he thought. Let them witness his fury unleashed. He would hunt down the crowd like a pack of dogs, so they would never again dare to create nobodies by doubting their own existence!

The watchman was standing behind him now. Through sleep-fogged eyes, he looked down at the village square, as the shadow of a watchman holding a rifle crossed the threshold, and fell across the crowd.

'What do you want?' cried the muhtar.

No one said a word. Everyone exchanged looks, as the crowd shrank back from the watchman's armed shadow and the muhtar's accusing voice. And perhaps that was when the villagers noticed the plane tree, and heard it rustling behind them; as fast as they could, they moved on past it, to return to their houses, throw open their doors, marvel in the sounds and smells of home, stroke their children's heads as they lay sleeping on their pillows, and cast their wives longing glances, before returning one by one to the village square to gather in front of the muhtar's office. The muhtar was still there, standing in the doorway. Now and again, Time's fingers grazed the tip of his cigarette as they passed him by. Whenever the embers burned, it took life from the crowd; whenever the embers died, it gave life back. And then those fingers let go of the muhtar's cigarette to pass over the crowd. It searched and searched until it had the shadow named Cennet in the palms of its moist hands. There followed the silent mystery of creation, as the hands pressed and tugged: they might have been a pair of blind and trembling sparrows, kneading something out of nothing.

The muhtar tossed his cigarette to the ground. He stamped it out. For a moment it seemed to him that the men standing before him, silent but for their breath, were not from this village. For they were all eyes, and nothing but eyes. Even their ears were eyes, now – their hands and mouths, too. Who could say where they'd come from, or how they'd arrived, these disembodied eyes? They must belong to the nobodies, who had sent their eyes ahead.

Whatever happened, it was the eyes that took the lead. On another night, after another ghastly disappearance, they'd bring their feet with them. Eyes needed feet, you see, which is why they were so often invited along. Later on, it would be ears raining down on the village square; great multitudes of ears, each doubting its own existence . . .

The watchman coughed. The crowd took this opportunity to move forward, as shapeless shadows slipped back in the direction of the plane tree.

'Please, Muhtar, listen . . .'

Anxiously, the watchman searched the crowd for the voice.

'I'm Cennet. Cennet,' said the same voice. 'I want my son back!'

The muhtar swallowed hard. Then he stepped back, to slam the door, on her and everything else.

17

The barber's apprentice had still not returned.

The barber was losing his patience. He kept going to look outside, and grumbling: this apprentice of his was as stupid as an ape. It was, I thought, like watching a ball of fire roll back and forth between the door and the chair. Now I could hear it roaring right next to me; now it seemed far away. It was outside the door, but also inside it. It was running up the street, while we sat on edge, awaiting its return. I was watching two barbers, through a single pair of eyes. It was making my head spin.

'He'll be here in no time,' I said, to calm him down. 'There's no need to get upset.'

'This is just not acceptable,' he murmured. 'It's not as if he had to go all the way to Fezzan. There are hundreds of markets along this street and they all sell razor blades. Just look at the state we're in!'

He pointed at the man in the chair, his face obscured by foam. If that was how you looked at it, then there wasn't any room for doubt. He was absolutely right. But I didn't want to tell him that. Not even in a whisper. Because I didn't want to say a word against the apprentice, who could, for all I knew, be just around the corner, running towards the shop, clutching those razor blades. And I couldn't bear for him to get the same drubbing as Cennet's son. So I didn't tell the barber he was right. I said something worse.

'Maybe he's not coming back.'

He turned those furious executioner's eyes on me. I fell into my chair, as if I'd been slapped. For a moment, I tried to think of some way to undo what I had said. But it was too late, for the barber was pacing the shop now, as he wrestled with the possibility that the apprentice might not return. I could hear the fury in the way he ground his teeth. He was using them, perhaps, to chew an imaginary apprentice.

Then he suddenly stopped.

In a deep, dark voice, he said, 'Please excuse me. But I have to go out now, to track down my apprentice.'

18

When Cennet's son emerged from the muhtar's office late the next morning, he was bent over double. He could barely put one foot in front of the other. But when he reached the village square, he made an effort to straighten himself out.

The watchman was just a few paces behind him; the muhtar had told him to be this boy's shadow, and to follow him wherever he went, in the hope that, sooner or later, he would lead them to Güvercin. This was more than an expectation. In fact, it was a must, now that the villagers were coming out in the middle of the night to crowd around the muhtar's office. That said, it was unthinkable that Cıngıl Nuri's disappearance had anything to do with Güvercin's: the two cases could not have been more different. Güvercin, after all, was a tender blossom, whose honour every villager from seven to seventy would protect. First in line was the muhtar, of course – of this the watchman was in no doubt. Just as he knew that he, too, was next in the list of likely suspects. But still he couldn't quite believe that the scrawny lad in front of him had it in him to kidnap this girl. They had made a mistake, that was clear, but after all that had happened, he couldn't bring himself to say so to the muhtar. What was done was done: the arrow had left the bow!

Cennet's son came to a stop. So did the watchman.

At every window was a villager, watching. Inside every courtyard, behind every chimney, outhouse and sack of chickpeas, there was a face, peeking out. The white-bearded old men sitting along the far wall were shielding their eyes from the sun and squinting – as if Cennet's son still had thousands of kilometres to cross before arriving. Perhaps, in their minds, they were all walking alongside him, waging the War of Independence. Hungry and thirsty and caked with blood . . . Leaving one battlefield in springtime, only to arrive at another.

At one point Cennet's son turned around to look at the watchman. He laughed. It was a strange laugh – unreadable – and the watchman was not sure how to respond.

How could anyone laugh, after such a beating? Could this mean that he was in fact the guilty party? It crossed the watchman's mind that this pimp might be making fun of him.

He stopped, without thinking, and lit a cigarette. Cennet's son was now entering his courtyard. He was still doubled up in pain. He staggered towards his mother, who had come out to meet him.

'Like a baby bear, running back to his mother,' thought the watchman.

He waited to see whether the lad would start laughing again. But Cennet's son didn't laugh; indeed he didn't even look back; instead he threw himself into his mother's arms. As odd as all this looked to the watchman, he slung his rifle over his shoulder and hurried back to the village square. Passing by the coffeehouse, he glanced through the dusty windows and caught sight of the proprietor. He had a steaming towel draped around his shoulders and was sucking on a cigarette, when their eyes met.

'Have you got any tea?' asked the watchman.

The proprietor raised his chin to indicate that he did not.

This despite the fact that the barber was sitting at one of the low tables, drinking tea. God only knew where he'd found it, but for the past few days he'd been wandering about with a cap pulled down over his ears. Now he'd lifted up the visor slightly, to listen to the radio that sat next to the partridge's cage. *Voices of the Nation's Choir Hour* was just coming to an end. There followed the strains of a wild folk dance, accompanied by madly clicking boxwood spoons that somehow made the coffee-house expand, until it was as large, and as loud, as a threshing floor. Then the saz players began to slacken. Each note lingered, like a drop of viscous amber, before dying away for the sly and spritely pipes, which jumped so high and swayed so low as to conjure up the folk dance itself, led by a man waving a triumphant handkerchief.

'Let me get you another tea,' said the proprietor.

'No, no,' said the barber, getting up. 'I have things to do; the shoemaker's waiting for me.'

Leaving the proprietor alone in the middle of the dance, he set off to see the shoemaker. The dog at the shop door greeted him with a snarl; it was a dirty yellow little thing, with teeth that called to mind a row of shrouded corpses. And that could explain why this cur was so interested in humans. Or so the barber thought, until he looked again at its filthy yellow fur, its callused paws, and wheeling tail. It was, he decided, no match for a man. But still a shudder went through him, as it opened its mouth wide to bark.

Looking inside, he saw the shoemaker beckoning. 'Come in, come in,' he said. The barber broke into a smile, and the bark got lost inside it.

The scent of hides made it difficult to breathe. They were hung one or two to a hook on the walls. Through the gloom he could see rows of old nylon shoes, and a pile of wooden heels. The shoemaker was sitting at the entrance on a cobwebbed mat, breaking in slippers with a fired iron rod.

'Did you hear?' he asked.

'Is there anyone who hasn't?' the barber replied.

They exchanged looks.

'Who do you think kidnapped Güvercin?'

'How would I know?' said the shoemaker. 'If you ask me, they beat up Cennet's son for nothing. The boy doesn't have the look of a kidnapper.'

'He's an odd one, though.'

'Let him be . . . The boy wouldn't hurt a fly. If he's odd, that's his business.'

Neither spoke.

'I don't think it was anyone from this village who kidnapped Güvercin,' said the shoemaker, after a pause. 'Because all the men are still here. I mean, even all the old men are still about. No one's found any excuse to leave.'

'Couldn't someone be hiding her somewhere here in the village?'

The shoemaker let out a discouraging laugh.

'You haven't been paying much attention,' he said, looking straight into the barber's eyes. 'They've searched this village from top to bottom.'

'When?'

'No time in particular . . . Would you even call it a search if they broadcast in advance? The muhtar made his investigations without anyone being the wiser. One person pops over to ask his neighbour for salt, another goes from house to house looking for pitch, a third goes from door to door asking for mallow. And so on, and so forth. Always a new excuse. They've looked every-where: everyone's accounted for. No stone has been left unturned.'

'They even searched my shop?' asked the barber.

'Of course . . .'

'But they didn't look behind the curtain, did they? I mean, where I sleep?'

'You may like to think so,' said the shoemaker. 'But when we went out for tea, didn't I reach behind the curtain for the glasses?'

That took the barber by surprise. How was it that the shoemaker knew every last detail of everything that happened in this village?

'So it was you?'

'Of course it was me . . .'

The shoemaker got up and went to get the tea glasses. The barber looked over at the iron rods, still molten red, and took a deep breath, recalling how Cennet's son had limped from the muhtar's office into the village square, doubled over and half dead, with the watchman a few paces behind, stopping whenever the boy stopped and walking when he walked, but faltering every time. Struggling, even, to keep his rifle straight, while the whitebeards leant drowsily against the wall, watching through narrowed eyes as the village came out in force, stepping one by one into the crowd encircling Cennet's son.

'You've drifted off,' said the shoemaker. The barber jumped. 'Aren't you going to ask me why I called you here?'

'Why did you call me here?'

'I've found you an apprentice,' said the shoemaker, holding out a glass of tea. 'As you know, Cıngıl Nuri has forgotten his trade . . . I don't think he'll ever hold a pair of scissors again in his life. To make a long story short, you're the only one left in the village who knows the trade. What'll happen when you go? Don't you think you need to take on an apprentice?'

'Of course I do,' said the barber. 'But how did you find someone just like that?'

'To be honest, he came of his own accord. He's at our place now, sleeping . . . The poor thing's been on

the road for days, and when he knocked on our door –
in the middle of the dawn call to prayer – he was
ready to drop. He's a distant relation, in fact. Comes
from a village the other side of the mountains. His
father gave him first to a barber in the city, and he
worked there for a year, more or less. I mean, he's
no longer green about these things; he's more or less
ready to go. Over there he would live and sleep in the
shop. Then one day, his master sent him to get some
razor blades or something, and he never went back.
Though it took him days, he went straight back to his
village. His father was pretty upset when he found
out what the boy had done. So he said, "If you're not
going to be a barber, then go and be a shoemaker,"
and sent him to me. But the boy's already done
time as a barber's apprentice . . . So I'm saying, why
doesn't he stay with us and we'll feed him, while you
teach him your ancient art?'

'I wouldn't mind that at all,' said the barber.

The twinkle in his eyes changed colour.

19

After the barber left, a deep silence fell over the shop. So deep, in fact, that it seemed as if many hours had passed since any noise had come in from the street, as if all the cars had come to a stop, and every workplace closed, and everyone outside was moving around on tiptoe, and I had been abandoned in this city of death, alone but for the man sleeping in the chair next to me.

And it crossed my mind that I should get up and leave this desolate and disordered place, which bore no resemblance to a real barber's shop, with customers who fled babbling nonsense instead of paying, or fell asleep with their faces lost in lather. It did not take me long to realise I could never do such a thing. Whatever happened, I was going to have to wait until the barber or his apprentice returned. This despite the fact that I knew the apprentice was never coming back with those razor blades. But I was sure that, after searching the streets, the barber would come back, huffing and puffing. And when he came in through the door, he would be looking for me, the person he'd left in charge of the shop. He'd look me in the eyes and take it all back. With a single look, it would all pass back into his hands. The scissors, the powder boxes, the cologne bottles, the brushes, the cotton balls and the mirrors – they would all be his.

The man sleeping in his chair still knew nothing of what had happened. When he'd closed his eyes, he'd been with a barber who was waiting for his apprentice to fetch some razor blades. As far as he knew, the barber was still sitting next to me; I couldn't abandon him. Leaving was therefore out of the question. It could well be that somewhere in my muddled mind, I was plotting out a novel I had yet to name. By which I mean to say that my mind had wandered many words – many pages – away from where I was sitting. And in that distant place, I could see a boy with flapping ears – a boy fashioned from my childhood memories, a boy who had yet to be born. But before I could work out what to do about this premature encounter, he had escaped my grasp, to occupy some other chapter. I was, nevertheless, confident that I could ferret him out, and consign him to his rightful place, some way after the book's last page, but something told me this wouldn't suffice. For all at once, a gust of mountain air rushed over me, bringing with it juniper-covered hills and mist-covered forests, lost valleys and bare slopes.

And with that, there was no question that this boy would continue to live, unborn, until the novel's last page.

20

When he walked into the barber's shop many weeks later, Cennet's son was shaking violently. Struggling to catch his breath, he asked in a wavering voice if Cıngıl Nuri could cut his hair.

'You know Nuri's given up this work,' said the barber.

But the boy refused to believe him. Waving his finger, he searched the shop for Nuri, sometimes laughing madly, and sometimes softly, only to burst into tears. The big-eared apprentice jumped up and went to hide behind the counter. Seeing that he had scared the child, Cennet's son stopped his searching and pointing, and plumped himself down in the barber's chair.

As he did so, he said, 'I saw Nuri only yesterday.'

The barber removed his white apron from the drawer. As he tied it on, he said, 'So, where did you see him?'

'Here, right where you're standing. He was shaving Rıza, first thing in the morning.'

'That was me,' said the barber.

'That wasn't you,' insisted Cennet's son. 'It wasn't you at all . . . It was Nuri. I talked with him.'

The barber had no idea how to respond to this.

His apprentice was confused too, in fact, and as he danced around the chair, he kept his eyes on the barber, to see what he would say. The barber, however, chose to remain silent. Nothing he could say would make the slightest difference. And that may be why he was able to finish the shave so quickly.

Without a word, Cennet's son got up and headed for the door. Then he stopped. He shook his head, which looked like a sad prickly pear. 'That means you must be Nuri,' he said.

The barber had to laugh.

And then Cennet's son rushed out of the shop, and into the village square. He opened his arms wide, as if trying to embrace the whole village, and bellowed, 'Why does the snooow faaallll?'

Passers-by slowed down to look at him. Doors flew open and slammed shut. The whitebeards leaning against the wall looked up and squinted, and then sank back again, to confer in whispers. As they always did, sitting in secret judgement of all that passed before them. But now they were at a loss, because so many things were happening that had never happened before. Each day, the list of things to discuss grew longer. Right now, for instance, a crowd of villagers had gathered in the shade of the plane tree. Slowly, very slowly, they were walking towards Cennet's son. Faces rose above every courtyard wall, children jumped out from behind every corner, every threshing floor and chimney. From every direction, they converged on the village square, forming a great and crooked circle, until suddenly, they stopped . . .

Cennet's son was going around the circle, asking each villager in turn, 'Why does the snooow, the snooow faaallll?'

No one answered. Some looked away. Others gazed at him in sorrow. Then somehow, the news reached Cennet, and she came running into the village square, her hair flying behind her. At first, it seemed as if she was going to put things right. In fact, all the signs were good; confronted with his dishevelled and bewildered mother, Cennet's son fell silent. But not for long. For now he broke through the circle to run at the plane tree. The circle stretched for a moment, as if tied to him by invisible thread, but in no time the crowd had begun running, with Cennet in tow.

Rıza the shopkeeper came out to watch, incurious and impassive. Cennet's son was now hugging the plane tree, screaming 'Why does the snow fall, the snow?' and kicking out at anyone who tried to approach him. Then he started spitting at them, and bursting into laughter, and babbling before finding someone new to spit at. Cennet was at her wits' end; stretching out her dry hands, she implored him to stop. Now and again, she'd turn around, seeking someone, anyone, who could help. And then, the muhtar strode in from wherever he'd been hiding. Eyes on fire, he walked straight over to the plane tree.

'You! Tell me, why does the snow fall?' shouted Cennet's son. The muhtar was silent. Then – much to everyone's surprise – he wheeled around and went straight back to his office, to collapse on to his desk. This was the end, he thought, as his conscience stung.

'Don't be too hard on the boy,' he said to the watchman, who had followed him in. 'He's lost his mind. He has no idea what he's saying . . .'

The watchman just shook his head. Dropping into a chair by the wall, he kept his sad eyes downcast.

'But to tell you the truth,' the muhtar mumbled, 'at this precise moment I wouldn't mind being in his shoes.'

Though even he had no idea where these words had come from. Or rather, he was sure he had not thought them: the words had just come out. After all these years of weighing every wise word, and watching many thousands of abandoned hopes settle into the creases of his lined face, he felt like an insect, crushed under its chosen burden, and flailing helplessly. And there he remained, deskbound and catatonic, until, without warning, a new idea came to him. Mulling it over, he walked to the window to look out on to the village square.

Cennet's son was still standing next to the plane tree, waving his arms about and talking to his mother. Unless he was shouting, and spraying spit, and asking, once again, why the snow fell. All the others had left the square by now, just about, to go back to their shops and household chores. Only Rıza remained. He stood in silence outside his shop, as if charged with the task of looking out for Cennet's son.

Watching from his window, and craning his neck, the muhtar felt himself go stiff again. Again, he felt a weight pressing down on him, a weight he could not move. He was stuck where he was, as helpless as a rusty nail that had been hammered into this window many centuries ago. His body hissed and hummed, but he could not move it.

Now and again, he murmured, 'So it's like that.'

The watchman stood by, pleading with his eyes. And with time, they worked their magic; the private muhtar sank away, to surrender to the public muhtar. Until at last, the two muhtars returned together to the desk.

'Yes,' he said again, 'it's like that. I've rumbled the rascal, at last!'

The watchman waited patiently for the muhtar to explain further. This he did not do. Instead he kept his eyes fixed on the bag containing his official seal, his mind on Cennet's son. Now even he had become an absence, it seemed. Albeit an absence of an entirely different sort. He had not vanished into thin air, like Soldier Hamdi, or come and gone like the pedlar, or slipped into the mountains like Fatma of the Mirrors, or flown off like Güvercin the Dove . . . Nor had he been propelled by inner turmoil to walk the earth like Cıngıl Nuri. He had, quite simply, become invisible to the naked eye. In this realm, at least. You could still see him every day, rushing here, there and everywhere. You could hear his voice and smell his scent, but without ever quite reaching him. This was, in effect, the cleverest ploy of all: to vanish into one's own mind. Maybe this was why Cennet's son had gone mad: so as to bury himself in his own thoughts. To succeed in going mad, he'd need more brains than the rest of them put together.

The muhtar pointed to the door. 'Go and fetch Cennet.'

His voice trailed off into the dusk. With some reluctance, the watchman went off to fetch Cennet, but she wasn't in the mood to hear what he had to say. She was still trying to persuade her son to let go of the plane tree and come home. Sometimes she went down on her knees to beg, sometimes she just ran back and forth, dodging her son's kicks, but she would not leave. After the watchman had followed her around the plane tree a few times, he repeated the muhtar's request. Cennet stopped; panting, she gave him a long look. Then she started spitting at him. The watchman was shocked. He made to reassure her, just to clear the air, but Cennet wasn't having it; raving, she shook her fists at him. He could not understand a word she was saying. She was growling like a dog. The watchman backed away, but this only gave her courage. Wiping the spit off his face, the watchman scrambled back towards the centre of the village square.

Before long, they were in front of the muhtar's office. The watchman, speechless and wide-eyed, seemed caught up in Cennet's shadow. The distance between them had not changed. But the time had come to bring this charmless dance to a close. Or so the watchman must have thought, as he scurried inside.

Still keeping her distance, Cennet paused, before letting fly a great wad of spit.

'Now they've both gone mad,' said the watchman.

Striking a match, he tried to light the candle next to the muhtar. Because the muhtar was sitting at his desk in utter darkness. At first glance, he seemed to be asleep, or even dead. When the candle was lit, his eyes were still closed. Then came a tapping at the window. The first thing the muhtar noticed when he opened his eyes were the pale portraits of Atatürk and Marshal Fevzi Çakmak. Then he read the bismillah on the back of the door, before turning his head to investigate the tapping. The watchman considered grabbing his rifle and running to the window, but somehow he found himself lying on the floor instead. Behind the glass, he could see a blurred face, fast approaching.

'That's Cennet's son,' whispered the watchman.

The face at the window went abruptly out of focus.

'Why does the snooow faaallll?'

The watchman shuddered.

'Let him be,' said the muhtar from where he sat. 'Let him shout all he wants.'

'Why does the snooow faaallll?'

The watchman slumped down into a chair, but he couldn't take his eyes off the face, not even for a moment. The same could be said of the muhtar, too: try as he might, he could not manage to ignore that nose pressed against the glass, or those grinding teeth. Many hours must have passed before they had stared this apparition into nothingness. Of course, it may well be that the face left of its own accord. Whatever the truth of the matter, the two men continued to stare at the empty window for some time afterwards.

When at last they stood up, they could hear Cennet's son in the distance. 'Why does the snooow faaallll?'

For a time, the watchman stood watching the muhtar making his way home, and then he crossed over to the other side of the village square. Slowing down as he passed beneath the rustling plane tree, he settled his gaze on Rıza's shop. Despite the late hour, there was light flickering inside. Sucking in his breath, he approached this window on tiptoes. Rıza was sitting behind the counter with two friends. On the tray in front of them was a wedge of cheese, a plate of pickles, three glasses, and a large bottle of rakı. The bottle was still filled to the neck, but it was clear that they were already deep in conversation: their hands were flying about, and when they weren't talking, they were puffing on their cigarettes. Every time they exhaled, their moustaches vanished in clouds of smoke. Then suddenly Rıza froze, as did the cloud of smoke encircling him.

'What's wrong?' the others asked.

'I thought I saw a face at the window,' said Rıza. 'It was looking straight at us.'

All three turned to the window to look.

'Why does the snooow faaallll?'

'The sound came from far off,' said one. 'It can't be Cennet's son.'

'Of course it's not him,' growled Rıza. 'You think he'd come here after kidnapping my niece?'

'Maybe you were just imagining things . . . If you look at a window too long, eventually you'll see a face. I mean, we all have one, don't we? A face we've lost, but are always seeking, even though we'll never see it again?'

'Never mind,' said the third. 'Where were we?'

'The two brothers.'

'Why does the snooow faaallll?'

Rıza started cutting the cheese into thin slices. 'So you were saying?'

'As I was saying, Gülbahar got two brothers to shoot each other . . . That's the way of whores; do they ever think of honour? When one brother left, the other arrived. They both knew what was going on, actually. They had to know. How can you hide anything in a village? Even if you do manage to hide something, how long can you keep it hidden? But as I was saying . . . The brothers soon worked out that they were both pissing on the same rock, and when they did, it became a competition. Who could bring her the finest delicacies, the best stockings, the most fabric? It heated up, this contest . . . When she saw all these presents, Gülbahar was well pleased, naturally, but she was left not knowing what to wear when she went out and about. Whenever she met up with the brothers, she'd wear all the gifts at once, so as not to upset either one.'

Rıza was eyeing a small slice of cheese. He was not listening to the story. He was thinking of Güvercin, desperately trying to conjure up her face, but to no avail. It was as though she had never existed, never once passed through this village. He could only remember her name: Güvercin. No hands or feet. No tongue, no lips. No shadow. Just a name. Güvercin...

'Why does the snooow faaallll?'

'And then?'

'Then one night, Gülbahar invited both the brothers to her home. They say she made a mistake, but I reckon it was the straightforward cunning of a whore! You know, I think the minx got bored of them both; every day the same-colour eyes, the same crooked nose, the same curly hair, the same smile ... And she said: I'll bring them both together and let them see what's what! In this game Gülbahar was playing, it wasn't clear who was the fire and who the tongs. But one thing's for sure, she didn't expect any blood, and certainly didn't think she'd be picking both of them off the floor at the same moment.'

Rıza was still looking at the small slice of cheese. He was concentrating so hard that he seemed to be spearing it with a mental fork. He read his whole life in that slice of cheese – his shop's fortunes, his son Ramazan's arrival, Güvercin's lost face – there was so much there that he was sure all he knew and loved would be destroyed, should one of the others eat it. He could take the precaution of putting it on a plate, and moving it out of reach, of course, or he could remove the danger by popping it into his mouth. Except that he wasn't after an easy fix. The cheese needed to stay where it was, untouched. Alas, it was not to be. Instead he watched aghast as it was snatched up and devoured. And Rıza let it happen. Oh where was it now, his slice of cheese? How he longed to tell them to stop talking about Gülbahar! But somehow he couldn't bring himself to speak.

'You drifted off?' asked the cheese-eater.

At the same moment, the watchman opened his eyes to find himself leaning against a courtyard wall at the other end of the village. He must have drifted off: his mind was still fogged. He could hear someone coughing on the other side of the wall, and someone else snoring. A baby was crying, the horses and cows wheezing. He thought he must be the only one still roaming the streets of the village. The others had long since blown out their candles and retired to bed. Only the old and the bedridden were still awake, and even they would be wrapping themselves up tight by now, to gaze mournfully at the ceiling, their ears against the wall, as the village sank into a silence darker than night itself.

The watchman had come to enjoy these moments, when every house, stable and courtyard in the village seemed his and his alone. The pretence of owning everything sent his thoughts to strange places. Sometimes, for instance, he imagined himself shooting people in their beds. Rıza came first, of course, and then Cennet's son, and Vehbi, whose courtyard stood next to his, followed by many others . . . However many he killed, no one would stand in his way. For everything in his dark and silent kingdom, from the newborn in their cradles to the last lost stalk of straw, was his and his alone. As he let his thoughts wander, he smoked his way through one pack of cigarettes, and then another, his rifle under his arm, his eyes never straying from Rıza's door. He could, he thought, be Azrael, the Archangel of Death. Until he had in fact become Azrael, to tower over the entire village. Knowing that he would continue to do so until morning, come what may, he'd point his rifle at a certain room on the ground floor of a certain house where Rıza's sleep was soon to be disturbed by a bullet flying into his hairy chest. As he marched towards his target, the rage inside him grew, until it felt as if a giant rope was pulling him forward. The click of an unpressed trigger shot through his hands as the roar of an unexploded rifle filled his ears, while in front of him was an unshot Rıza, gaping like a baby bird.

'Why does the snooow faaallll?'

Slowly the watchman got back on his feet. This madman, he thought, was not going to let up all night. He came to a stop at Rıza's courtyard gate. Peering through the windows and cracks in the door, he tried to catch a glimpse of those sleeping inside. Not a sound in the village: not even the grass crunched. He pushed the gate open and tiptoed inside. There the darkness seemed even darker. But never mind: he knew where the stable door was, and now he crept towards it on the tips of his toes.

'Where have you been?' Hacer whispered.

Prepared though he was for any eventuality, the watchman jumped. 'I'm here now, aren't I?'

'Where is he?'

'He's in the shop, drinking.'

They climbed into the hay.

'I suppose you don't know what's been happening in the village, then,' said the watchman sternly.

'How could I not know?' asked Hacer. 'But listen. It's been ages since you've come to see me.'

'Is Ramazan asleep?'

'He is.'

'He's got a lot bigger, hasn't he?'

'A lot bigger. He's become a fine young man.'

The watchman took his rifle off his shoulder and placed it within easy reach. Hacer was lying in the hay, breathlessly awaiting him, but even after all these years, she still kept throwing glances in all directions, for fear of being caught. The watchman crouched down beside her. Taking her hands in his, his mind went blank. Meek as a kitten, he stretched himself out, as the village sank deeper into its silence, with its houses and courtyards, and the clatter and clutter of daylight receded into the blank beyond. Until there was no one left on this earth but the watchman, and Hacer of course, as they fell unseen into the dark and silent abyss. Wasting no time, Hacer pulled up her skirts to receive the watchman, who had already pulled down his trousers and was shuffling towards her on his knees, safe in the knowledge that he was no longer the watchman, but the great and towering Azrael, flashing his executioner's eyes. He began by caressing her legs. Then suddenly he tightened his grip, as if to yank them off. As she struggled to free herself, her great thighs strayed. He sank his teeth into her nipples and was wild with joy when she screamed in pain. Now fury overtook him. He attacked the writhing Hacer like a rabid dog. He even growled as he bit into her lips, which soon began to swell, like honeycombs. They had just reached the melting point when suddenly they stopped. The watchman hurled himself across the hay, as if in response to the rattle of a gun. And there, for a time, he stayed, shivering in the darkness.

By the time he got up to put on his trousers, he was no longer the great and fearsome Azrael. Once again, he was the watchman, flashing his bright white teeth.

'Come again.'

'You're trying to say I won't?'

'Come more often.'

'I will, but first we need to get rid of this curse.'

'What curse?'

'What curse! Are you blind? Everyone in this village keeps going missing.'

Hacer said nothing. She felt around for the rifle and when she found it, she gave it to the watchman.

'Have you ever heard of Soldier Hamdi?'

'I've heard the name. Wasn't he the scoundrel with the nine wives?'

'Exactly! Where are his children, eh? And where, for that matter, are all those courtyards, bursting with all the children he squired?'

'How should I know?' said Hacer crossly. 'They are where they are!'

'But I'm serious,' said the watchman. 'So listen . . . They must have been born under our noses, and they must live under our noses, but now, with all these disappearances, we can't even see them.'

When they reached the stable door, the watchman paused to think. He was about to ask Hacer a question: 'What if we can't see any of this because we don't exist either?' But a warm goodbye kiss stemmed his words.

'Come again,' said Hacer.

He said nothing. Quietly, very quietly, he crept across the courtyard. Heart on fire, he strode off without thinking where he was going. Suddenly, out of nowhere, a shadow came to block his way. There it stood, glaring down at him with imperious impatience. Hoping to slip by unnoticed, the watchman moved towards the wall. But now, with a great leap, the shadow did the same.

'Why does the snooow faaallll?'

'Get the hell away from me!' the watchman cried.

Cennet's son went wheeling off – first in a zigzag, and then in a circle, and then jumping from one side of the road to the other, faster and faster, a bit of silver here and a bit of silver there, flashing like a drop of mercury, cackling horribly all the while.

And the watchman just stood there, not knowing what to do. He felt angry. He felt cornered. But at the same time he knew there was no moving forward.

Slowly, very slowly, he raised his rifle, to take aim at the laughter.

21

The man who had been sleeping in the chair now opened his eyes and looked blearily into the mirror. It was clear he had forgotten where he was. When he saw the lather on his face, he seemed shocked.

I didn't know for sure what time he woke up. When I noticed him looking into the mirror, he still seemed deep in sleep. His face, his form – they seemed so far away. With every laboured breath, that distance seemed to increase. Perhaps he had mistaken the reflection in the mirror for the real world. Perhaps he had been trying to find a foothold in the receding silence. I cannot say how long this lasted. But when he emerged once more through sleep's fine curtain – when his eyes found mine in the mirror – the shop itself seemed to shudder. In some strange way, everyone and everything slipped out of place. As the light glinted off the pair of scissors on the counter, I saw them click shut. The bristles left their brushes to fly up into the air, while the powder boxes rattled.

And then, as suddenly as it had begun, it ended. But the silence had been broken. The traffic in the streets began to hum again, the people on the pavements began to move. And the man in the chair began to talk.

'When are you going to shave me?'

He'd turned to look at me. I was, of course, surprised. Too surprised to speak.

'As you know,' I said, after a long pause, 'I'm not the barber.'

He screwed up his face. I could see he did not believe me. And I could tell, from the fire in his eyes, that he was not a little angry.

'Don't joke about,' he said now. 'I've got things to do. I've got to get back on my motorbike and go.'

'I'm not joking. I'm not the barber. I'm just a customer who came to this shop after you. But I suppose you know that already. I think you're the one having a laugh.'

'But how could that be?' he cried in astonishment. 'What are you implying – that I dropped off for a few moments, and lost my mind?'

'It wasn't a few moments. You've been sleeping for at least an hour. Maybe even an hour and a half.'

At this, he fell silent. Leaning back into his chair, he watched me through half-open eyes. He was trying to look fierce, but I could tell my words had shaken him.

'Why don't we try to go back to the beginning?' I suggested finally. 'Why don't you tell me how you came to be here today, and what happened next? It might help us shine some light on all this.'

He was so lost in thought now that I wondered if he might have drifted off to sleep again. 'I came here by motorbike,' he murmured. 'I wanted a shave before I set off for the village. Half an hour ago, when I came through that door, you were trimming the moustache of a little man whose hair had grown into his beard. I said hello, of course . . . Then I waited for a while in that chair where you're sitting now. Then the little man jumped up and left . . . I don't even think he paid. In fact, as he was leaving, he muttered something about a skeleton outside. I came and sat in the chair in his place, but I must have drifted off a little . . .'

'And the apprentice?'

'What apprentice?'

'Was there no apprentice in the shop? I mean, a little boy with flapping ears who danced around the chair with little clipped steps while the barber was shaving the customers?'

'No,' he said, carefully, 'I didn't see an apprentice.' Again he fell silent. I watched him try and make sense of his surroundings, as with every new breath his fear grew.

There was no need for me to ask if he could remember me coming into the shop after him.

'You must have been dreaming,' I announced. 'You must have had a dream while you were asleep.'

He flinched, as if I'd insulted him.

'Look, let me explain,' I continued. 'For one thing, what you've said doesn't fit. You claim that all this happened half an hour ago, but you've been asleep for at least an hour, or maybe even an hour and a half. You think I'm the barber, and his apprentice, too. This is ridiculous. As everything we dream about always is. My guess is that some real memories found their way into your dreams, and then you forgot you were dreaming. It happens to us all.'

He searched my face, as if to find something he'd lost. And I was sure I had not convinced him. It occurred to me then that perhaps he had no choice but to be silent, to lean back into his seat and await the barber's return. In this I was mistaken, for now he asked, 'What do you think? What if everything you and I have said just now happened in a dream?'

22

The muhtar was sitting at his desk, shakily smoking a cigarette as he inspected the bloodstains on the skirting board. So long as they were there, Cennet's son would be there in the office with them. The muhtar could almost see – almost feel – the boy's eyes on him. Darting glances, lighter than silk, but how they weighed on him, how they pinned him down. Beads of sweat were forming on his forehead, and on his hands, as he tightened his grip on his chair. And this might have been why he did not hear the knock on the door. Or rather, he heard unseen hands hitting against an unseen door, flailing in the darkness, trying, without hope, to force open the lock.

A second knock, followed by an angry kick, and the door swung open.

'Give me my son!' cried Cennet.

Picking up his amber prayer beads, the muhtar gave her a wan look.

'Why don't you tell me? Where is he?'

'You know full well where he is! He hasn't been home for three days. What have you done with him?'

The rest the muhtar could make no sense of, so he sat back in his chair and let the words wash over him. It was clear from her mouth that the woman was speaking. From time to time she stopped to point at the wall, or the door, or to ask a question. After each question she would look straight into the muhtar's eyes, awaiting his answer. When no answer came, she would revert to the waving and the shouting. The muhtar wanted to think that he saw what she saw, but as he saw it all without hearing what she said, he couldn't be entirely sure. Cennet's son had already absented himself from his own existence. If, as this woman was saying, even that absence had gone missing, then the situation was very grave indeed. The way things were going, he would be waking up one morning to find that the entire village had gone missing. Maybe it had already done so, and no one had noticed. Maybe no one had noticed because no one in the village saw anything strange in someone vanishing . . . In which case, Cennet could have vanished into thin air just by living in their midst, by fading away like they all did, as their faces and voices grew pale and faint, and their scent floated away. Each breath they took was shallower than the last, but still no one noticed. Not even when their nearest and dearest disappeared did they notice! And if that was the case, then there was nothing they could do to remedy the situation. It was far too late, the muhtar told himself. There was no way out . . . If only they had paid more attention at the outset, they might have found a way to keep the entire village from absenting itself. But now it had gone too far and everything that had made the village what it once had been – the women and children, the animals, courtyards, trees, and earthen rooftops, the sounds and smells and smiles and aches – had vanished into a giant void where one absence sat nestled inside another, without ever realising that they were no longer there . . .

Shouting and screaming and waving her arms, Cennet advanced on the desk. She didn't seem to mind whether he understood what she was saying or not. Then suddenly she fell silent. At that moment, she looked tired enough to fall on the floor in a heap. A minute later, she turned on her heel. And once she had left the muhtar's office, it was as if she had never been there.

The muhtar stayed put. There was no point in moving. He would not have known what to do, or what to say, or how to behave. He knew only that a great despair had settled on the village, with every new misfortune only adding to it. That said, when Cennet's son had gone mad, the villagers had been so busy trying to explain his strange behaviour that they'd pretty much forgotten about Güvercin. It was true that Reşit still came to his office once every two days to ask if there was any news of his daughter, only to bow his head and shed a few tears. More than a few, in fact. Usually it was so bad that Rıza had to come over to take him home; he'd have fallen from his chair by then. He'd have to be carried like a snivelling sack across the village square, damning every living soul, right until the moment he reached his bed. Passing through the courtyard gate, he would leave behind him a trail of rakı-flavoured obscenities. With time, the villagers tired of his antics, but still no one had the heart to say so. It was the opinion of the white-bearded old men resting at the foot of the wall that Rıza should simply put a bullet through the forehead of whoever kidnapped his niece and put an end to it, knowing that, in any case, Reşit would eventually calm down.

Without warning, the muhtar jumped up, as if it had at last come to him what he should do. Leaving his office, he walked straight to the barber shop. All the villagers sitting under the plane tree seemed to be watching him; a few passing horsemen slowed down, just a bit, as did a dilapidated ox-cart. And this was why the muhtar decided that when he reached the barber shop he would wheel around to give them a meaningful look. But when he saw the boy at the door, he stopped dead in his tracks.

'Who are you?' he asked in a deathly tone.

'The apprentice,' replied the boy.

The barber emerged from behind a curtain to watch.

'I didn't know you'd taken on an apprentice,' said the muhtar. 'Whose son is this?'

As the barber walked towards him, he seemed not to believe his eyes.

'The boy's not new,' he said. 'He's been here a long time.'

'How long is that?'

'Goodness, it must be four or five months by now. You must have seen him.'

'But he wasn't here the other times I came?'

'He was,' said the barber.

He said this with such conviction that the muhtar lost his nerve. He did not dare ask again whose son this apprentice was. Instead he fell clumsily into one of the chairs in front of the mirror. Once settled, he leant back to contemplate his reflection, but when he locked eyes with the apprentice, he looked away.

'If he was here,' he murmured, 'then he must have been here.'

Best, he thought, not to ask whose boy this was. Best to change the subject, he thought, as he tugged at a drawer.

'Cut my hair very short,' said the muhtar. 'And shave off my beard, but make it clean.'

Nodding, the barber took up his scissors and began cutting. Fixing his eyes on his master's hands, the apprentice began to dance around the chair with tiny clipped steps.

'Planning any travel anytime soon?' asked the barber. The muhtar, already half asleep, looked up.

'Travel where?' he asked.

'Into the city,' said the barber.

He left it at that. There was no need to ask why he might wish to go into the city. For the rest of his shave, he said nothing; it was enough, he thought, to glare into the mirror. When the towel around his neck was removed, he leant forward to examine his face. Then he turned to look at the back of his neck. He gave it a few strokes. Then he moistened his fingers and set about fixing his eyebrows. The barber had never seen him so neatly turned-out before, and perhaps that was why he looked him over with such interest as he handed him his cap. But the muhtar paid him no attention: he was still arranging his cap. You'd think he was off to a wedding.

Without another word, he went back through the village square. But not in his usual way: he seemed to be sleepwalking. The villagers sitting under the plane tree whispered amongst themselves as they took a good long look. Rıza was with them, or rather, some way off from the others, drinking Turkish coffee. But the muhtar saw none of this. He was walking into parts unknown. His mind raced ahead, his body loped behind. To the white-bearded men at the foot of the wall, it was clear that – however high he held up his head – the mind inside was in shreds.

He walked the length and breadth of the village that day, leaving no street unvisited, no courtyard untouched, no corner unturned, or fountain untested. Wherever the villagers went, they found him. Some, who had only ever seen him on a few occasions, now found themselves greeting him in several different places, several times an hour. The barber thought he must have somehow managed to multiply himself. Considering the grim countenance of each and every one of the many hundreds of muhtars now roaming the streets, they would surely multiply even further. Not all of the muhtars were the same, either; one would have a faint smile as he greeted the villagers he passed, another would pass them without a word.

As the evening sank into darkness, one of the silent muhtars planted himself outside Reşit's courtyard gate. Sucking in his breath, he glared and stared. Then he tiptoed forward a few paces. He could have taken this moment to scour the courtyard for any clues he might have missed a few months earlier, but the very thought struck him as absurd. Nothing in the yard had changed; that much was clear from the stale scent at the doorstep, the length of the shadows and the width of the walls. All that could be said was that if Güvercin had left a trace here, it was now far off in the past.

Just then a horse whinnied in the stable to his right, its eyes flashing like silver pebbles. The muhtar jumped. For a moment he thought it might be Cennet's son, playing his second disappearing trick. As he neared the stable door, he tried to banish the thought. After all that had happened, Cennet's son would be staying well away from Reşit's house. Pushing open the door, he peered through the horse's ripe breath, passing his eyes over the straw-strewn floor, the bags of pinecones piled against the wall, and the feedbags hanging from the rafters. Every few moments, the horse would prick its ears to look up at the sky, but nothing else moved.

Now Reşit was racing down the stairs in his bright-white underclothes, to stand before the muhtar. Or rather, to stoop, because his back was as bent as the rafters. After a silence that seemed to last hours, the two men set out together for the cherry orchard. They might have been puppets, played by the same hands, for they turned their heads in synchrony. If one stopped without warning, the other stopped too; if one jumped, so did the other. Stopping in the dark night to savour the scent of cherries, the muhtar began to whisper. Reşit hung his head, straining to understand his words.

At this same moment, another of the muhtars was back in his office, sitting at his desk. He was gazing again at the candlelit bloodstains on the skirting board, and waiting for the watchman, who had gone off to fetch him a horse. As quiet as he looked now, this muhtar had been busy preparing the horse that the watchman was now bringing over. His wife had come with him to the stable, and slipped some food into the saddlebag. She had then settled herself at the door, to fix him with a mournful look. She was waiting for an explanation, but the muhtar paid no heed to her silent pleas; he was righting the stir-rups, tugging at the horse's mane and adjusting the saddle.

When he found the strength to take his eyes from the bloodstains on the skirting board, they came to rest on the portrait of Atatürk. While they exchanged quiet glances, the muhtar asked himself if time had stopped; as unwilling as he might be to entertain that possibility, he suspected that it had. But if that was the case, then the time had come to restore it.

So he reached into the innards of his waistcoat and retrieved his seal. He placed it on the desk in front of him, while a wordless Atatürk looked on.

'I've brought the horse,' said the watchman.

He stood up, gave the room one last gloomy once-over, and blew out the candle. Another muhtar, at least as gloomy as he, had long ago locked the door and made his way to the horse at the foot of the flag-pole. The watchman, brought up short by the pace of events, stumbled behind him.

'Are you ready to go?' he asked.

The muhtar laid claim to the horse's reins, gripping them tight. 'There's no other way,' he said.

He paid no attention to the watchman, or the door of his office, the horse's heels or the village nestling in darkness; instead he gazed into the far distance. And then he gazed beyond that, to the place those living there would see if they, too, gazed into the far distance, and in that spirit he began his wanderings.

'Don't take down the flag,' came his voice from afar. 'Keep it up until I come home!'

The watchman nodded. The muhtar loosened the impatient horse's bridle to allow it to take a quick bow.

'And don't try to open my office. I've locked the door.'

'Have you got the key with you?'

'Yes, I have!'

'Fine, then,' mumbled the watchman.

The muhtar spurred the horse and it leapt towards the darkness. Just as it was vanishing from sight, he came to an abrupt stop. The muhtar leant back, clinging to the reins. The watchman, thinking he'd forgotten something, took up his rifle and raced off towards him. But as he neared, there was again the echo of horses' hooves. The muhtar was leaning down to say something to the watchman. He seemed about to dismount, to dash back through the night to his office. Then suddenly a second horse emerged from behind the watchman. Sitting on its back was another upright muhtar.

'In all honesty,' he asked the watchman, 'why *does* the snow fall?'

23

The man in the chair was staring deep into the mirror, as if he were still dreaming. It made him tired, just to see how tired he looked. At the same time, he was sure that if he took his eyes off the mirror, he would probably fall asleep again. This time he would dream of puttering over the mountains on a motorcycle, crossing the plains in search of a village that the world had forgotten. But its inhabitants had not forgotten him; some were watching the road, some dreaming of the road and some whispering of their memories of his last visit.

'I have to go,' he said.

I wasn't completely sure that he had spoken. Because the voice I heard was far away, and as weak as a clumsy sentence. Each word was its own phantom. Maybe the man in the chair had only thought these words. Maybe I was still waiting for him to say them. I took a deep breath and looked at him, waiting for him to repeat them.

'I have to go,' he said again.

'Where?' I asked. With sleep-fogged eyes, he gazed at my reflection in the mirror.

'You said you had to go somewhere?'

This made him laugh. I was, I feared, the object of a joke I had yet to understand.

'I didn't say anything of the sort,' he snapped.

That took me aback. I decided I must have angered him when I'd said he'd been dreaming. Now this was his revenge. Because the moment he worked out that I wasn't sure what I had heard, the ghost of a smirk crossed his face.

'You never said you had to go?' I asked again.

'No,' he said, 'I never did.'

'Fine, but what was the last thing you said to me?'

'I said maybe this conversation we're having right now is nothing but a dream.'

Then silence. At a loss, I looked back into the mirror.

He was scraping the foam off his face, but that ghost of a smirk was still there. Yes, most definitely. He was enjoying his revenge.

'Don't be upset,' he said next, in a voice that was both childish and grave. 'I didn't say I was going, but I *am* going. I can't waste any more time waiting for this barber.'

Though I did not wish to cause more trouble, I decided to ask him where he was going, one last time. But for some reason, I couldn't coax the words from my mouth. And once again, it seemed as if he could hear what I hadn't said, for he gave me a watery grin as he leant down into the sink to wash his face. What was this contest that bound us together? It had no name, though it had us eyeing and goading each other. Whatever we said, it turned into a game of wits.

As he rose from the chair, he pulled the towel off his neck to dry his face.

In a soft voice, I asked, 'What do you do for a living?'

'I'm a postman,' he said, gesturing towards the motorcycle parked outside. 'Actually, I detest that word . . . I prefer "herald" . . . I like having a motor-cycle, of course.'

He draped his towel over the back of the chair. Moving to the door, he looked at his watch.

'Are you off then?'

'Yes.'

'You've left it too late,' I said. 'You might as well not go.'

He turned to look at his motorcycle.

'How could you ever know how late I was?' he said stubbornly. 'I need to go.'

24

A few days after the muhtar rode off into the city, Cennet's son came down from the mountains carrying a jet-black snake. He acted as if he'd never been lost, but with his hair growing into his beard, he seemed to blur at the edges, like a ghost. Entering the village he paid no attention to the children running along behind him; he had eyes only for the snake in his arms. Sometimes he would mumble a few incomprehensible words, sometimes he would stroke its head, only to shiver and look back up at the cliffs. It was almost as if he had spent his lost days in the mountains wrestling snakes, and now had a whole nest of them after him, seeking their revenge, for he watched his back as if his life depended on it.

By now there was a huge crowd of children trailing him. The white-bearded old men at the foot of the wall agreed that there was absolutely no difference between this return and Cıngıl Nuri's all those years ago. But it did not surprise them. Life always insisted on repeating itself: the same play with different actors, as time passed by . . . But this time, there was no shiny paper or shredded tinfoil. Instead there was a jet-black snake. There was Cennet's son, in Nuri's body. As for those noisy boys – they were reliving the legend that their older siblings had passed down to them. Now it was their turn to find the fear in their curiosity. For everything about Cennet's son, from the way he moved to the way his hair grew into his beard, made him Cıngıl Nuri's replica, so much so that they were tempted to bring Nuri down to the village square, to show him how he had looked all those years ago, on the day of his return.

But this was not to be, for the children didn't give them the chance; instead they formed a tight ring around Cennet's son, their voices rising and rising as they trailed him from street to street with an ever-growing clamour. By the time they reached the coffeehouse in the village square they might have been an army. Cennet's son paused for a moment. With a raised arm, he signalled for the boys to stop. Which they did, then and there. Then, following his lead, they dropped to the ground, forming a large circle. No one made a sound. Except for the few who rubbed the backs of their hands in the dirt, to scrape off the snot, no one moved, or even breathed, as they fed their curiosity on the man in their midst. He returned the compliment, examining each face, as if in search of something he had lost. Then, as the boys shivered and gasped, he straightened out the snake as if it were some sort of scarf, and wound it around his neck. The snake raised its head, thrust out its flickering tongue, until one of the boys could no longer stand it.

'Woouuuoooow!' he shouted.

And it was as if they had all been waiting for this cue, for now the boys began to shout and stamp their feet. The noise travelled all the way to Cıngıl Nuri's house, and then past this house, to the mill and then the cemetery. When the villagers reached the village square, all they could see was a ghostly cloud of dust. Plunging into it, they fought their way past the children to get to Cennet's son. Even the old men who had been watching from the sidelines now walked one by one, bones rattling, into the fray. But once they had done so, they formed a separate group, watching in silence as everyone else laughed at Cennet's son – laughed at him hard.

And then, without warning, Cennet's son shook off the snake. They all held their breath in expectation of another special trick. It was all so sudden that those who had been bent over laughing remained bent over, even as they gave the snake their undivided attention. Everyone, from those who had come out of the coffeehouse to those who had come running from the fields, was standing shoulder to shoulder, trying to find out what they had missed.

Before long, they heard an engine puttering in the distance. First the watchman and then the rest of the village forgot all about Cennet's son. Instead they turned in the direction of the mill, to watch a yellow motorcycle racing towards them down the winding roads until at last it came to a halt in the middle of their own crowded village square. The man who now put one foot on the ground was the postman. His hair had grown into his beard. He asked for the muhtar, just as he had done so many years earlier.

'He's gone to the city,' said the watchman. 'Whatever you've brought, you can give it to me.'

Glaring at the children who were pawing his motorbike, the postman reached into the saddle. With a grand flourish, he pulled out a dusty letter. All eyes were glued. All ears strained to know what news he'd brought. Even Rıza, who had been drinking heavily since the day his niece was kidnapped, swearing at anyone who had the temerity to come near, even he pushed his way through the crowd, hoping that the postman had brought news of Güvercin.

'Stop playing games. Just read it!' he blurted, his voice heavily flavoured with rakı. The watchman said nothing; folding the letter, he put it into his pocket and walked towards the plane tree. Then a thought came to him, or so it seemed. He wheeled around and looked at the postman, still perched on his motorcycle, leaning on one leg. But every time the watchman blinked, the postman seemed to be riding back into the village. So he danced around the plane tree, coming to a rest in the place where he'd begun, with a final stamp of the foot.

'Rest your weary feet, my friend,' he said. 'Get off that bike of yours and drink some of our tea!' The postman stroked his beard for a while and gazed at the great crowd of boys. If he left them to watch over his motorcycle while he drank his tea, he'd be too far away to keep an eye.

'No,' he said, 'I have to go.'

A few others tried to insist, but the postman wouldn't change his mind. He had to press down on the kickstarter a few times before the motorcycle sprang to life. Suddenly, his head flew back and the motorcycle shot forward. He took one more quick loop around the children and the plane tree, and then he was gone. Shielding their eyes from the sun, the villagers watched him slip past the mill, to disappear in a cloud of dust.

Cennet's son was left all alone with his snake outside the coffeehouse, entertaining a crowd of imaginary spectators. Some time later, when the children had tired of the departing motorcycle, they again crowded around him to watch. The villagers, meanwhile, sat beneath the plane tree, watching the watchman.

'Just read it,' said Rıza.

The watchman opened up the letter as slowly as he could, thinking it might be from the muhtar. Mouth firmly shut, he read it to himself first. Then he paused to think, very deeply. But then, his shoulders started shaking. He began to laugh, while the villagers around him exchanged quizzical looks.

'You take it,' said the watchman to Cıngıl Nuri. 'Look, this telegram mentions you. Your relatives came back from reporting you missing many years ago, but this telegram has only just arrived. How splendid is that! And look, it says that they still haven't been able to find you!'

Now everyone was laughing. Nuri seized the telegram, not knowing what to do with it. He looked up at the watchman and let out a strange little giggle.

'Look at the good work God has done,' said the imam. 'He has changed painful news into a source of great mirth . . .'

The villagers nodded. Nuri folded the telegram and slipped it into his pocket, as carefully as if it were an official certificate of absence. Still smiling, he sat down.

'Get up,' said the watchman, crossing his legs. 'Get up and get us a tray of tea – we should drink to this news!'

'I don't know who you're talking to. I've still not been found,' smirked Nuri. 'I'm lost! If you like, I can show you documentation!'

'I don't want to see it, get up and get the tea!'

Still smiling, Nuri got up.

'None for me,' mumbled the imam.

He stood up and walked towards the barber shop, snapping his prayer beads all the way. His shadow took the shape of a dark creature. The imam considered for a moment if there might be nothing left on this earth but the shadow cast upon the earth by the first to walk it. A chill passed through him. Just the thought of it frightened him – just the idea of it. He muttered a quick prayer.

When he came through the door, the barber was sitting by himself. His ears were still ringing from the puttering motorcycle. So, too, were mine.

25

And a chill went through me, for it seemed that the imam had come to the city barber shop rather than the one in the village. Though he brought the village square with him. It was hard to believe he wasn't still there, in his chair by the wall, his hands carefully placed upon his knees, slowly clicking his prayer beads while his blank eyes wandered. At one point we locked eyes. But he seemed so far away – from the shop, and from himself – that I chose to remain still and silent. I did not even dare blink. For I knew that he was here to share my solitude. I had no choice but to sit here saying nothing until his shadow receded.

So there I sat, waiting; I waited for what seemed like hours, watching the cars and the crowds in the streets roll past, only to return as phantoms in the mirror, only to vanish into nowhere with the jagged glints of light bouncing off the scissors and the silent taps, until only the imam remained. By now, I had, to some extent, become him. When I left the barber shop to make my way back to the village square, I was wearing a confused frown.

My shadow followed on behind me, of course. But it kept pulling me back. Heavy as a dead bear, it was. So heavy that I was soon wondering how long I could keep it up. But somehow I managed to walk past the plane tree, and the villagers sitting underneath, and Cennet's son, who was still performing for the children gathered around him, and a few ox-carts piled high with chick-peas, and the white-bearded old men at the foot of the wall. Until at last I had arrived at Rıza's shop.

I found Rıza at the counter, holding an almost-finished glass of rakı in his hands, as he talked to his son Ramazan.

'You saw it with your own eyes,' he said, pointing at the road the postman had taken. 'There's still no news of Güvercin!'

Ramazan nodded, and the shop seemed to darken. Perhaps they didn't intend it, but father and son drew closer together as the night and the scents of soap and grease closed in on them. While I lingered at the door – erasing myself, almost – as I absorbed their words.

'Your Uncle Reşit doesn't have a brain in his head! For months now, I've been saying we should go and talk to the imam. I said it so often, the words burned the hair off my tongue, but would he listen? The man's as stubborn as a goat . . . I'm telling you, the imam doesn't make mistakes about this kind of thing. Even if he did, let's not forget that he was the one who found Cıngıl Nuri all those years ago. Well, not exactly. But you know what I mean. Even if Nuri returned to the village all by himself. We were arguing about this again today; I didn't exactly say that it was God's doing but I put aside my respect for your aunt, and said what I thought! Then your aunt pitched in, saying their girl would never be found if all they did was doze like dogs around the muhtar's office. They owed it to themselves to go and see the imam, just this once.'

'And what did my uncle say to that?'

'Well what do you think? He blew his fuse!'

Ramazan sat down on a drum of sunflower oil to gaze at the beams on the ceiling.

'Why don't we go instead?'

'Go where?'

'To the imam.'

Rıza's eyes went as red as two grapes as he turned away to take a deep breath.

'We can't,' he said, after taking a large mouthful of rakı. 'Don't you understand? It has to be the guardians of the lost person that go to the imam. Her father should go, or her mother . . . When the imam fills his bowl with holy water and looks at it in the mirror, they'll be able to see where she's hiding . . . If this was as easy as you seem to think, don't you think I wouldn't have done it by now?'

'All right, so what do we do?' said Ramazan, biting his lip.

Rıza took another gulp of rakı.

'There's no other way. We have to convince Reşit,' he murmured, wiping his mouth with his hand. 'I've already told him so. I've told him the time has come for him to see what the imam can do.'

'How are you going to make *that* happen?'

Rıza leant over the counter.

'We decided this together,' he said in a whisper. 'We thought and we thought, until we came up with this ploy. So listen to me. In a few minutes, you will go and pay Reşit a visit. He'll give you a hair. Then you'll pocket the hair and go straight to the imam's door. Tell him you've fallen in love, all right? Say you are at your wits' end . . . You can't eat, you can't drink, and you can't stay still. Whatever you do, you can't get that girl out of your mind. You've got to spin a mighty tale, you hear? Talk about your dreams and your daydreams, and the fire burning inside you, really lay it on . . . Whatever you do, stay serious. We can't have him wising up. Keep your eyes on the

prize! Just go in there and kiss his hand and tell him
how you're suffering . . .'

'And then?'

'Then the imam will ask for the hair of the girl
you've become infatuated with.'

'How do you know?'

'I know, because that's how these things are done.'

'Are you sure?'

'Of course I am. Then he'll start blowing on the
hair. He'll make the girl it came from fall in love with
you. Not only that – she'll fall so deeply for you that
she'll come and stand outside our house bleating for
you. And at that moment Reşit will see what the imam
can do!'

Ramazan gave him a sidelong look.

'That's all fine and good,' he said dubiously. 'But
who's the girl?'

Rıza gave his son a stern frown; downing his glass,
he slammed it on the counter.

'You're a bit slow, my boy,' he said. 'If we knew
who the girl was, we'd never be able to convince
Reşit that the imam did it, would we?'

Ramazan looked helplessly at the floor. The shop
fell quiet, as the funk of soap and grease grew thicker
and the darkness deepened. Soon they were no longer
father and son, but executioner and victim. And then,
without warning, Rıza stood up to pace behind the

counter. Every now and again, he would throw his son a suspicious glance.

As for me, I was still in the doorway, leaning against the jamb. But there seemed to be no point in waiting any longer, so I slowly entered the shop. Weaving my way past between the drums of paraffin, the bags of soap, and the glass candles hanging from nails on the wall, I headed for the counter.

'Look, it's the barber,' said Rıza to his son. 'Go and order us some tea!'

26

As the imam drifted off to sleep, his hands stayed awake, leaping from the ground to the divan, and from there to his knees, like two enormous frogs. A knock at the door made them jump just enough to disrupt the shadows. The imam sat up. Muttering a few bismillahs, he pulled up his socks and made for the door. While opening the latch, he gave so long a bismillah that even God himself was surprised.

There, on the doorstep, stood Ramazan, his face dark with worry.

Together they made their way through a series of half-lit rooms, each one adorned with bunches of dried thyme. Arriving at last in the darkest, dankest of them all, they sat down on a low bed. On the opposite wall hung a portrait of the sainted Ali, sparkling like the desert sun against a background of heavenly green. Sinking back into the straw cushions, Ramazan could look at nothing else, for it seemed as if Zulfiqar, his legendary sword, was pointing straight at his forehead.

'Welcome,' said the imam.

Ramazan kissed his hand and leant back again. He clasped his hands, gazing up at the sainted Ali as if to ask for his assistance in escaping the plot he'd been forced into. He had no choice but to take the plot a step forward. The imam was watching his every move.

'You have a problem,' he said.

'I do,' Ramazan replied.

Saying this, he took his eyes off the sainted Ali to sigh deeply. It wasn't fake, this sigh, and it occurred to him that he had unwittingly made himself more convincing. Though of course he had reached the point where anything he felt would make him more convincing.

'And?' said the imam. 'Won't you tell me what's wrong?'

'I've fallen in love, sir, that's my problem . . .'

The imam rested his chin on his chest, playing with his prayer beads, as if Ramazan had not even spoken. He looked so unconcerned that Ramazan feared the man had seen through him. Though it wasn't just fear he felt then: half of him hoped that the imam would foil the plot his father and uncle had foisted on him.

'To love is to reach the highest state of being,' said the imam suddenly. 'How wonderful that you have reached it . . .'

'But the girl doesn't love me.'

The imam raised his head to smile sweetly at the window.

'There are remedies for that,' he said gravely. 'You need only to bring me a few hairs from the girl's head, and the rest is simple!'

Ramazan gulped.

'I c-c-c-ame prepared,' he stammered. 'I have the hairs with me.'

The imam dropped his prayer beads and lurched forward, as if to grab a stray wind before it left again.

'Then give them to me,' he said, stretching out his hand. 'Hand them over!'

Reaching into his pocket to pull out the napkin in which he had wrapped the hairs, Ramazan glanced up at the sainted Ali. It was almost as if he were in the room with them. This only added to the tension.

'They're very short,' grumbled the imam as he opened up the napkin.

Ramazan looked down despairingly. Meanwhile, the imam was slowly turning his back on him, bending over double to examine the hair in his right palm. To look at him, you would think he was staring into a deep well; his eyes grew ever wider as they bored into their black depths. He muttered a few prayers, or rather, he whistled them – no doubt to bring some light into that dark abyss. These prayers grew longer, until it seemed to Ramazan that the imam would soon melt into them and disappear.

But he didn't. Instead he sat there, hour after irksome hour, never moving his eyes as he prayed.

At last he stopped . . .

'My task is completed,' he said in a tired voice. 'Carry this hair with you wherever you go. From now on, the girl will love you back, until you are as close as the water is to the soil.'

'When will it start working?' asked Ramazan.

'That's up to God, my son. I can't say a time for sure. If his loyal servant is truly certain of his love, then the fire will surely be spreading to the girl's heart too . . . We've just made the spark, with God's blessing: maybe it will take a month for the fire to catch, but it might have already happened by the time you step through my door . . .'

Ramazan refolded the napkin with care before putting it back into his pocket. An odd and unexpected shiver passed through his heart, as though somewhere inside it a match had just been struck. He gave the imam a pained look, as if he could already feel that small flame searing him. Then he came back to himself, and leant over to kiss the imam's hand again with genuine gratitude.

'You have nothing to worry about,' murmured the imam.

One after the other, they rose from the divan. As they passed back through the dim and thyme-scented rooms, the imam bent over to pull up his socks. At that same moment, Ramazan caught sight of a black cat peering in through a door that had been left ajar. Its eyes were burning like embers. Ramazan wanted nothing more than to narrow the distance between them, but it was not to be: he had no choice but to follow the imam from room to room.

But as he made his way from the imam's house to the village square, he could still feel the cat's eyes burning inside him. And perhaps this was why, though he went right past it, he failed to notice the crowd of boys that was howling with laughter as Cennet's son did more tricks with his snake.

Entering the shop, he found his father behind the counter, drinking rakı.

'All done?' he asked hopefully.

'All done,' said Ramazan.

Rıza leant back against his rough shelves, which were black with dust. He let out a great sigh of relief.

'So it's done,' he said edgily. 'Now go and tell Uncle Reşit!'

Ramazan shuffled out of the shop, mute as a lamb. Embarking on what he knew to be the most direct route to Reşit's house, he kept wondering if he had lost his way. When at last he stopped, he felt as if he'd aged years in a matter of hours. Each step he took forward was slacker than the last, and the orders his head was issuing didn't translate to his legs. Struggling to point himself in the right direction, he found himself back in the village square, but this time he didn't notice Cennet's son either. He was too busy trying to put one foot in front of the other, and wondering which of the girls of the village the hair might belong to. No one on earth but Uncle Reşit knew who it was and yet a shiver went through him each time he passed a girl in the street. It did not escape his notice that a number of the black-haired girls let their eyes linger, to cast him longing glances.

Just then, fifteen or twenty paces from the barber shop, he caught sight of the barber, standing at the window, gazing out at the village square. A moment arrived when he saw Ramazan, but his eyes slipped away, as fast as sun slipping across his window. It slipped across that window to hit the barber in the eyes, flooding his shop with a dark red light that oozed through the door and into the village square. It was at that very moment, in a doorway darkened by that shining light, that Ramazan caught sight of the cat whose eyes burned like embers. His legs melted beneath him as he feasted his eyes, in rapt concentration. It seemed to count his steps, then it used its paws to toy with its ears, and then, at long last, it gravely turned its head.

When he reached the end of the street, Ramazan's heart still ached. He turned around to steal another look. The cat's eyes were still following him. Although far, far away, they were bright with a light that lightly tripped over the stink of soil to mingle with swallows in flight and the mid-afternoon sun as they silently approached.

Turning the corner, Ramazan walked as fast as his feet would take him. Though the cat was far behind him now, it still seemed to be watching him, through each and every wall he passed. With this thought, he sped up. Then he tried to slow down, but to no avail. This strange cat was teasing him, that much was clear. As often as it moved, it stood still. It had powers and motives he could not begin to fathom. It was playing with him, just like his father and his uncle, and the more he struggled to free himself, the deeper he sank. By the time he reached Reşit's courtyard gate he was completely out of breath. If he could only calm down and collect himself, this absurd game of tag – that could be real, or could be a dream – might come to an end, restoring him to gentle laughter as life returned to normal. But this proved impossible: he could not for the life of him catch his breath. He kept huffing and puffing, faster and faster, while his chest began to rattle, just behind the pocket in which he had hidden the hairs.

Somewhere nearby, a horse let out a neigh, sharp and clear. He breathed in, just as sharply, and pricked up his ears, but all he could hear in the ensuing silence were hornets buzzing and birds singing.

He pushed open the gate and crept in. When the wooden latch fell into place behind him, he was struck by a great wave of regret: he had no idea why, but his regret was overwhelming, pulsing through his body, gripping him like a vice. He took another few steps towards the stairs in the corner, then heard the neighing again. This time, it was a lot closer. He turned towards the stable door and timidly advanced. All of a sudden he noticed the horse's eyes flashing like silver pebbles; flaring its nostrils to submerge him in its warmth. And there it stood in the darkness, stamping its feet while it modestly bent its head, as though it knew it was being watched. It kept letting out short whinnies, as if to tell him something. Ramazan, meanwhile, stood there transfixed, his eyes caught by those flashing pebbles.

Then, with an enormous smash, the horse broke through the door. Faster than an arrow it circled the yard, rearing up with its ears still pricked.

Ramazan was stunned. His first thought was to run and catch it: maybe this is why he opened up his arms and jerked a few paces forward. But the horse reared up again, crushing a cheeping chick as it descended. Ramazan staggered back blindly until his back was pressed against the courtyard wall. He opened his eyes to look in horror at a pair of horseshoes and a gaping yellow-toothed mouth . . . Rather than trying to catch the beast, he was thinking now of how to escape its hooves. The stairs were in the far corner of the courtyard. He would never reach it in time. As he watched the horse furiously pawing the ground, it occurred to him that there was no time for anything. Then he realised that he was leaning on a door; and before he could feel surprise at his good fortune, he was hurling himself through it.

Reşit, hearing the commotion, came rattling down the stairs, arms akimbo. But he couldn't stop the horse from bounding over the courtyard wall. He reached the courtyard in time to see a black tail vanishing. He ran as far as the gate, through a cloud of desperate, flapping, squawking chickens. He looked out into the street. Nothing.

Ramazan, meanwhile, was still running away from hooves he could hear pounding behind him. The horse was now a fierce black wind, raging through the village, street after street. Huddled in the shadows of the old men by the walls, the boys of the village found outrageous pleasure in the sight of a horse chasing Ramazan. But the whitebeards were as worried as those who watched from behind their courtyard walls. Ramazan couldn't even see them: if ever he turned his head, he was met by a cloud of dust.

Cennet's son was sitting in the village square at that point, trying to find a new way to entertain the many boys and assorted men who were not as amazed as they had been when he wrapped the snake around his neck like a scarf, or kissed it, or wound it through his belt loops to hold up his trousers. When he first spotted Ramazan, with a sable horse in fast pursuit, he paused. He failed to notice that the snake had slipped from his hands and was now twisting through the soil. In the blink of an eye, it was already beyond his grasp, hissing as it headed towards the boys, who now ran off screaming and running in all directions. Taken by surprise, Cennet's son did not know where to look. Should he watch the horse as it raced after a terrified Ramazan, or the dust cloud the crowd were running into, or the snake slipping through it? In any case, he seemed to have given up on catching the snake, or eating, or drinking or asking why the snow fell; indeed, he even seemed not to be breathing.

Suddenly a crowd of men rushed out of the coffee-house, pushing and shoving.

'What's happening?' shouted one.

He pointed towards the panic-stricken crowd.

The others stopped to look.

Ramazan, bent over double, was still running from the horse. The sky above was alive with pounding of horses' hooves, which kept changing direction, like an ill wind. The horse's whinnies, meanwhile, bounded off the walls of the village square and did not appear to be slowing. No one moved. No one exchanged looks, or a single word. They might have been dead, for they could not touch, or run, or scream.

But then, sight restored, they could see it as it happened: Ramazan's knees giving way, and Ramazan on all fours, Ramazan crawling across the ground, as if possessed. The horse towering over him, rearing higher than ever before, to bring its forelegs down on him, neighing with an animal – even lustful – abandon that was beyond human understanding. The village square shuddered with the sound of bones cracking. As those cracked bones began to spray blood, the boys ran home to their courtyards.

But Ramazan, writhing beneath the horse's hooves, could not follow them . . . He couldn't even scream, unless he screamed so violently that no one could bear to hear . . .

Finally, after an eternity that no man could measure, the horse stopped.

The earth below was so red it might have been a poppy field. For a short while, the horse contemplated the bloodstains. Then, as the village square came back to life, it listened. Then it picked its way through the scattered flesh and bones, pausing now and again to sniff Ramazan's blood.

And this was when the villagers took action. In silence, and as if in keeping with a well-made plan, they fanned out in an arc to catch the horse. But the moment the horse saw them, it reared up, rising several times on its hind legs before galloping off.

The village gasped as one . . .

Rıza slammed down his rakı. Ashen-faced, he raced out of his shop. Seeing the blood, he stopped short. Seeing his son, he stared in horror, and collapsed.

On hearing the news at her courtyard gate, and even before she saw the ribs jutting from Ramazan's chest, or the teeth sticking from his cheek, or the fast-clotting lake of blood around him, Hacer fainted.

27

Once again I was alone in the sighing silence of the barber's shop. By now I had given up on the barber and his apprentice; as I sat next to the window and watched the passing traffic, my thoughts wandered off to that faraway village.

In fact I had no choice in the matter. For by now they were all inside me. Güvercin, who was still nowhere to be found. Cennet's mad son, who wanted to know why the snow fell. The watchman. Rıza. The imam who didn't know which girl's hair he had enchanted. The muhtar who had still not managed to return from the city. Cıngıl Nuri, who still could not say where he'd gone all those years ago, or where he had returned from. Reşit, who wandered between his house and the muhtar's office and back like a rickety old skeleton. Hacer, whose smouldering skin set the stable aflame, and Ramazan, who was crushed by the horse: they were all inside me, just as I was inside them. Which meant, perhaps, that I might also be the girl from whom Reşit had asked for a lock of hair, that my name was Güldeben, that I was sitting on the divan next to the window, looking across the roof-tops to the wooden minaret, recalling the night just past. The night I'd cut off a lock of my hair – my hair, that was as black as sorrow – and dropped it into Reşit's hand . . .

I did not know that the imam would soon be blowing on it, nor did I know whose heart it was that his muttered prayers would link with mine. The old man Reşit had simply told me to cut off a lock of hair for him, no questions asked. It happened at dusk, at the courtyard gate; he was squatting on the ground, fixing me with those little eyes of his, in which tears were still drying. Since losing his daughter Güvercin, he'd been a ruined man. And in all honesty, I could not understand why he would wish to pay a visit to a little unlucky stay-at-home girl like me. I supposed he was looking to take his mind off things. I was also worried about who the man on the other end of this might be; I feared he might be blind or bedridden or crippled or hunchbacked or a widower as old as my grandfather. But he allayed my fears: he told me that my father knew and that I should trust him – the man I would fall in love with was one in a million, as handsome and presentable and golden-hearted as a young man could be . . . If he told me his name it wouldn't happen; and anyway, it was just a bit of nonsense, this thing Reşit was going to do. It might work, it might not; either way, it was for God to decide . . . But if everything went according to plan, I would have no problem finding out who he was. I'd find him for sure: the fire inside me would lead me closer to him, day by day. Those coals smouldering in my heart might even land me on his doorstep, bleating like a lamb. The man would go through all this as well, of course . . . If he failed to breathe in the smoke from my fire, if those flames failed to engulf him, it would all come to naught; and if that proved to be the case, the one carrying the fire would perish . . . If it were me, I would go wandering like Mecnun, the crazed lover who scoured the deserts for his love until the flames consumed him . . .

It was only yesterday, in the half-light of dusk, that old Reşit fixed his puffy little eyes on me and told me all this. And I was still Güldeben, sitting on my divan by the window and thinking of that man. After all that has happened since, Reşit will never want to tell me who it was. Even if he wanted to, he would never find the strength.

And yet, I knew: I had fallen in love with a dead man.

28

They buried Ramazan that same day, following the afternoon prayers. This was the first death the barber had seen in his few months in the village, but he remained silent throughout the funeral. He walked with the others, and looked just as sad; he rushed to pick up the coffin, threw some soil on the grave, and poured a little water from the tankard being passed around. Beside him was Reşit, also silent. Eyes downcast, and Adam's apple bobbing, he propped up Rıza, who was weak from crying. He was so deep in thought that he didn't even notice Rıza hiccuping drunkenly at his shoulder.

Lagging behind them was the ashen-faced, fast-withering watchman. It was almost as if he was lagging behind his own rifle. As he struggled to complete Ramazan's last journey, he looked over and above the sea of heads in front of him, to fix his eyes on the mountains. Even if he could have found the strength, he'd not be pressing his tear-soaked lips against this coffin, to release the secret he'd held inside for so long. It was far too late for that. Ramazan had died believing a lie about his birth, and that was how he would be buried.

Once again, the watchman prayed that it would be all over soon; this mournful walk behind the coffin, the saying of prayers and the throwing of soil, the pouring of water and the standing in silence. The imam, meanwhile, was struggling to believe that the boy who had been his guest at the break of dawn was now dead. He was walking so slowly it didn't even look like he was moving, and every now and again he came to a full stop. With every prayer, he felt more distant – from the villagers gathered at the grave, and the village itself, lying in silence beyond the almond grove, and its houses, and what was yet to come. If Reşit had not let go of Rıza's arm to jump, sobbing, into the grave, the imam might have drifted yet further away. But circumstances having intervened, he clutched his robes, and rushed over to rescue Reşit, whispering a few desperate words of solace into his ear as he led him through the crowd towards the cemetery gate.

By the time they got back to the village, night had fallen. One by one, the candles were being lit. Without saying a word, the villagers gathered under the plane tree to listen to the silence of the village square. Raw with grief, they stared at the spot where Ramazan had lost his life, as again they heard a horse galloping through the afternoon. They could see the dust rising, almost. And a body, curled up into a ball, in a pool of blood and bone. As the children drifted off to sleep in their beds, their mothers and fathers drifted back to that afternoon, as the blood spilled again.

Then the imam offered Rıza his condolences. The others followed suit. This was the most difficult part for the watchman: as his turn neared, he tried to stop himself from quaking. But to no avail; his whole body was quaking, and with a violence that was impossible to hide. At last it was Cıngıl Nuri's turn, and then it was his; throwing his arms around Rıza, he closed his eyes and sobbed. And then it was as if the two grief-stricken men were slowly melting into each other, until all that was left was one great mouth crying out into the darkness. When he let go of Rıza, the watchman felt as if he'd been torn in two. He adjusted his rifle, which had slipped from his shoulder.

United by darkness, the leaves on the plane tree sighed, as slowly the crowd dispersed.

'I hardly have the strength to walk,' whispered Reşit to the watchman. 'You take Rıza home.'

The watchman nodded.

'This is their time now,' Reşit said. 'If I go, I'll be even worse. I don't know what I'd say to Hacer.'

The watchman took Rıza by the arm and on they walked. He didn't know what he would say to Hacer either. They'd lain together in the stable many hundreds of times over the years, but now he was afraid to see her. If he'd had a place to go, he'd have fled this village then and there, so as never to come face to face with her again. No chance of coming home years later like Cıngıl Nuri. As he led the sobbing, sighing Rıza back to Hacer, it occurred to him that such escapes were impossible. And then he was angry at Reşit, for forcing him to confront Hacer before a single day had passed.

Reşit, meanwhile, had somehow recovered his strength. He had gone ahead, and was now marching furiously up his steps. He stopped now and again to cry, 'Is anybody there?' But his voice just bounced off the walls of the empty rooms. In a rage now, Reşit ran through the house, climbed up on a divan, seized the rifle from the War of Independence years, took it off the wall, and headed straight for the stairs. He had panicked for some reason, and now, for some other reason, he'd set his mind on completing a task he'd put off for far too long. But by the time he reached the top of the stairs, he'd lost his resolve. Setting down his rifle, he lay down on the floor.

Once he'd caught his breath, he knew he had no choice but to shoot the horse. No longer could he give this beast so much as a handful of feed or a mouthful of water, no longer could he stroke its mane or slap its rump. No longer could he look it in the eye and not see Ramazan, writhing at its feet. Each and every time, this image would return to burn another hole in his heart. Each time, he would imagine Ramazan disowning that pool of blood and cracked bones, and slowly rising from underneath that horse. But never would he come closer. He would just stand there, accusing Reşit with his eyes.

Reşit stood up. He was loading his gun as he came down the stairs. Once in the courtyard, he stopped to look around him. Those little eyes darted left and right at random. Hours later, when his wife came home, having put poor, exhausted Hacer to bed, she found him standing in the same place.

'Did you see the horse?' asked Reşit.

She glanced first at the rifle, and then at the stable. 'Isn't it in there?'

'No.'

'Then let it go to hell!' she said.

'Didn't you see it on your way home?'

'I didn't,' she said, as she climbed the stairs. 'I wasn't at home when it happened. I came running as soon as I heard!'

Reşit was still standing below her, mumbling in the centre of the yard. He fell silent when his wife came back down the stairs.

'I'm going over to see my brother,' she said. 'I think I'll stay there overnight.'

'Then go,' mumbled Reşit.

But he himself went nowhere that night. He didn't even go inside to eat or drink. He just stood there as the courtyard slowly darkened. He hoped that, sooner or later, the horse would return to the stable it had lived in for years. In fact, this was more a wish than a hope.

But by the time a distant rooster announced the impending dawn, it was less a wish than a fantasy. And by sunrise, Reşit, still waiting at the courtyard gate, had replayed this fantasy so many times in his mind that it turned, once again, into a consoling hope.

With that, the sleepless man took his rifle out into the street, going from door to door to ask all the villagers if they'd seen the horse. No one had seen it since it had squashed Ramazan like a grape, but no one wanted to turn Reşit away hopeless, so they all tried to conjure up a couple of words. Most shared stories of the crazed, wide-eyed horse they'd seen racing after Ramazan, trampling him as they watched. The horse they described was enough even to dishearten Reşit: a dragon, black as night, racing faster than the wind, gaining speed each time they told the story.

Those who hadn't been in the square when Ramazan was trampled spoke of hearing a horse galloping past Cıngıl Nuri's house to head straight for the cliffs. For a while, they could hear the horse's bloodcurdling echo in the thyme-scented afternoon sun. This had given way to hours of anguished whinnying. The horse was still there, in the shadows of the cliffs, possibly on a precipice, if not in a valley. Wherever it was, it was still stained with blood; it had nowhere to go but the village it could still see in the corner of its eyes. It looked almost like a human being, there in the juniper bushes, hiding out of shame in a darkness tinged with green, shedding great tears, and heaving great sighs . . .

Some of those who had heard the horse galloping away spoke of the noise resounding through the village as it raced across the fields; some went so far as to imagine which paths it had taken. Reşit didn't know who to believe; the confusion that had stalled him all night long now returned, as he wandered through the village. Then Rıza joined him. He had heard that his brother was looking to shoot the horse. Together they set out for the cliffs, holding rifles in one hand and revolvers in the other.

Reşit wasn't at all happy with this, in fact. He wanted to find the horse himself, whatever the cost, and put a bullet in its head on his own.

29

I was still sitting alone in the chair by the window.
I could no longer see the cars passing by; after
hours of speeding up, they had, by nightfall, lost their
shape and colour. Now they were buzzing past the
barber-shop window like phantom flies.

I was, at the same time, with Güldeben at her
window, fearful of having fallen in love with a corpse,
so I wasn't prepared to believe that the cars outside
my own window had disappeared entirely. They
might, I imagined, have melted into their surroundings. So much of what I could see from here bore a
resemblance to cars, after all: the apartment blocks
lining the street, for example, and their satellite
dishes, the balconies, the entrances of office buildings,
the people pouring out on to the pavement, and –
most of all – the ones venturing on to the pedestrian
crossings . . . Now that everything out there had

mingled with everything else, it was clear that even the cars were no longer just cars: look into their windows and you saw the city reflected and deflected. My eyes resting on a car window, I would suddenly be presented with an apartment façade, for example – or a distant window, shimmering all the colours of the rainbow, but I could not be sure if I was in front of it or behind. The window was probably covered in dust, the windowsill blackened over time by exhaust fumes, but the occasional shaft of evening light still found its way in. And when it did, the city in the window ceased to exist. And every building it had ever reflected went smashing into every other, until they were one with the families inside them. Watching all this from the barber-shop window, I was frightened, of course: I was sitting in a city that was melting before my eyes. I had just one branch left to cling to, and its name was terror.

After the city had rebuilt itself, only to collapse again, and then rebuild itself, a hundred times over, I noticed someone standing at that window. He was very tall, and because he was standing at the far edge, he might have been mistaken for a curtain. He might have been there from the time I first came in for a shave, but if he had the eyes of an executioner, they were too far away to see. Nevertheless, I was sure of it, because this man in the apartment on the third floor of the building across from me was gazing so far into the distance that he seemed to have left behind his body. I was shaken myself, of course, as I still did not know if I was inside that window or outside it. With this in mind, I lowered my eyes.

Maybe the window I could see was not the same on both sides; a view could change, depending on where you were standing, and how you felt. And there was no clear rule about whether you should look out or in: if your eyes permitted, you could do both at once. No doubt this man had found himself in this same situation; whatever he saw when he gazed out of that window he also saw himself, as far away, and as close, as in a dream . . . It could well be that he had met with this surprise before I had. For somehow, it must be true, but who would want to believe that the person he had come face to face with was himself?

Which was all well and good, but what of the person on the other side of the window? Did he genuinely believe he had gone beyond himself?

30

At midnight there was a knock on the door. The barber, who had been sleeping on his sofa all evening, first mistook it for a dream, so he turned over and buried his face in his pillow. He was just drifting off to sleep when there was another sharp knock. The barber rose drowsily, felt around for a match, lit a candle, and fished under the sofa for his slippers. Gazing at the rose-print curtains that separated the front of the shop from the back, he wondered who could be knocking on his door at this time of night. As he padded across the floor, he heard a sound, but it wasn't his slippers squeaking; it was something outside. Through bleary eyes, he looked out of the window. The shadow at the door looked back.

'Who is it?' asked the barber.

The shadow wheeled around to vanish into the darkness. The barber took his candle closer to the window, trying to work out who it could be, but all he could see in the glass was a barber leaning forward to peer through the window. This unsettled him; without thinking, he began buttoning up his shirt. Then he put on his shoes, and began to march, as if setting off on a long journey, though the shop was only a few paces across. He had not felt like this since his first days in the village, when he was still longing for that city he'd left so far behind, and he tried to remember how it had been for him, in that other barber shop, on that busy street. In bits and pieces it returned to him, though he couldn't quite conjure it back to life. All he could see was a vast sea of apartments, crashing against the horizon; the cars flying off the streets to crash through windows. This was just a dream, he told himself: a dust-ball of memory and disintegrating hope. All the same, it fired up his desire to be elsewhere, so off he went towards the city of his dreams. Hour after hour, he walked . . .

Until his energy was spent. Hearing a rooster crowing at the other end of the village, he sat down on the divan, and told himself how tired he was. But there was no one there to hear his words. How dark the shop was, and how quiet. It seemed larger than ever. So did the silence, and the barber's sense of it.

The barber lit a cigarette, taking a deep drag as he looked around him. Then he wondered how many others there were in the world, sitting just as he was. How absurd, he thought, to worry about something like this, yet he couldn't help thinking of the thousands of others who were sitting just like he was, deep in thought. In his mind's eye, he watched those thousands of others in thousands of other rooms, all striking the same pose. These thousands of bodies, he told himself, were the bridges that would lead them to the future. Each one its own strange creation with no other concern but to walk the same paths; unknowingly repeating the same repetitions, the same gestures, the same smiles, the same gait, and the same way of sitting, fired up by the same spirit of adventure while they all walked in place.

The barber took another pull on his cigarette. His eyelids drooped as he thought about those thousands of others, sitting just as he was, at that same moment.

There were thousands of watchmen, no doubt. They'd have walked far from their villages, to stop off at cabins like the one where Fatma of the Mirrors and Soldier Hamdi settled their scores, and now they were sitting there, striking exactly the same pose as the barber. He felt as tired as them, too: since the day Ramazan was buried, he'd hardly slept. He'd had no choice in the matter, actually: wherever he looked, he saw a flying black mane. The horse might have gone, but its ghost still haunted their streets; it would gallop in from the night, tail waving, and stop right in front of him, almost as if to mock him, or it did a few laps and vanished. A few days after the bloody scene in the village square, the watchman began to imagine walking through the night, and suddenly catching sight of the horse – wandering the streets, wandering the fields. Indeed, he had prepared himself for that very eventuality; first he would stop dead in his tracks for a few moments, just to give the horse a chance. Then he would approach it on tiptoes to stroke its nose. Finally he would place the barrel of the gun under its chin, and fire. The horse would rear up when the bullet hit its brain, of course, but then would fall to the ground, spurting blood that the night would hide from view. It might wave its tail a while, or kick its legs, or try to get up, but before long it would be curling up to die. And that would be that – the watchman would leave it for the vultures that circled the cliffs. As the beggar-birds gorged, he would pray for Ramazan's soul . . .

But as it happened, no one saw the horse in the days that followed. Morning and night, Reşit wandered across mountains and valleys. Some nights, to go further afield, he lingered with the goatherds in the upper pastures, but he couldn't find a thing. For a few days, Rıza followed close behind with his revolver, and then grew tired, saying his heart was still aching, almost making it clear that this was a barb aimed at Reşit for going off on his own to search for the horse. But there was more to it than an unspoken reproach, for the pain of losing Ramazan had made him even fonder of rakı. From morning until night he kept the shop open, and kept drinking.

Even though he knew all this, the watchman never went to see Hacer again after Ramazan died: whenever he found himself approaching Rıza's house in the dark of night, he wheeled around and went a different way. Their days in the stable were over; the time had come to forget.

The watchman lit a cigarette, narrowing his eyes as he took a deep drag, striking just the same pose as the barber. Then he broke that pose, to pick up his rifle and walk in the direction of the cemetery. Without thinking, he jumped over piles of stones that came up to his knees, and discarded bits of mattresses, and wads of wool, abandoned kites, scrapped tin stoves and bones of unknown animals. He wove his way between the graves. Each mound resembled a child sleeping under a blanket of soil. It was just before daybreak when he collapsed to cry in silence on Ramazan's grave. He could not say what had brought him here, or what he had hoped to achieve. Dropping his rifle on the ground, he went to knock on the grave, as though the decomposing Ramazan might still be breathing, and preparing to leap from the earth. Much, much later, a moment arrived when the smell of death brought him the promise of sleep; had Reşit's horse arrived at that moment, he would not have found the strength to stand up. A quick glance to either side. Then he lay down next to Ramazan and closed his eyes.

He fell into such a deep sleep that it was almost noon when he awoke, covered in clammy sweat. He felt as light as a bird now and as he made his way towards the cemetery gate, it did not feel as if he were walking over soil fed by the dead. He might have been a bird walking across clouds. He wondered if he was still asleep, if it was only in his dreams that he'd awoken, as he neared the village's first houses. He was passed by creaking carts on their way to the mill, and their weary oxen, and horse carriages, and ghostly donkeys, and rakish foals with eyes that danced like boats on a turbulent lake, and in the far distance men, women and children, but he didn't see a single one. They were all behind the curtain that protects dreams from the real world. Then suddenly everything was a lot nearer. The muhtar's office came into view; holding his snake in one hand, Cennet's son was pummelling its door with the other.

'No one's there,' he shouted. Cennet's son turned to look at him.

'There is,' he said, narrowing his eyes.

'Don't punch the door for nothing,' said the watchman. 'The muhtar locked it when he went into the city, and he took the key with him!'

Shaking his head, Cennet's son walked away.

'I suppose you're right,' he murmured. 'Or so I suppose. But you know what, Mr Watchman . . . I think someone's in there, believe it or not . . . But even if there's no one, think of this. This village square has started to smell!'

The watchman glanced at the snake on the boy's arm before attempting a smile. In this he failed, for now he pressed his lips, as if he had just smelt something bad as well. He traced out little circles, as his nose took him to the source.

Then Reşit appeared at the end of the road. The watchman sat down, placing his rifle across his lap, and watched with bleary eyes as Reşit approached. It was, he thought, like watching an actor walk on to the stage, for he was the spectator: the others appeared to pay him no attention.

'Can you smell something strange?' asked the watchman. Reşit looked around him, with narrowed eyes.

'It's odd,' he said, stepping out of character. 'It seems there is a smell, but what is it?'

Cennet's son was on the ground, flapping his legs, trying to coax the snake to slide off them. But he, too, had been watching this strange play from the wings, in secret.

'Reşit,' he shouted. 'Psst . . . Reşit!'

Red-faced, Reşit wheeled around to look, as fast as if to keep a second Reşit from running away.

'I didn't kidnap your daughter,' said Cennet's son. Silence, until he cried out, 'Neither did my snake. Thought I'd let you know!'

Reşit walked off, leaving Cennet's son behind him, along with the watchman, the muhtar's office, the village square and the strange smell. Without thinking where he was going, or why, he went wandering through the streets, passing courtyard gates, and sacks of chickpeas, and ox-carts, and horses, carts and the children . . . As he walked, he wept. He wept until his insides had shrunk to the size of a baby's hand. With each painful step, his rifle grew heavier. But still Reşit walked on, through narrow streets where Güvercin and Ramazan were both present in their absence. And so he went, in pursuit of a phantom horse. Reaching the edge of the village, he walked on to the cabin where Fatma of the Mirrors and Soldier Hamdi had settled their scores. But as everyone knows, every cabin has an orchard, and every orchard a mulberry tree and every mulberry tree birds. Even the walls and the doors of this house had been repaired. There were curtains now, too. And printed on those curtains were flowers and branches that fluttered and swayed in the breeze passing between them. Reşit stumbled forward through the vines, until he stopped to catch his breath and look in wonderment at all the changes, as proud as if he had made them with his own hands. Then he spotted something moving behind the window, or rather he felt it, sensed it . . . Leaning on the courtyard wall he craned his neck to see more. An impossibly beautiful girl was sitting on the divan, looking through the mulberry trees, gazing down at the village, with its wooden minaret. Deep in thought she was, deeper than the ocean . . . She was as beautiful, he thought, as Fatma of the Mirrors . . . She, too, looked weary, as though sentenced to wait here without ever lifting a finger.

'Look over here,' said Reşit.

The girl awoke from her beauty and stood up.

She, a verdant cypress, leant towards the window. Peering through the bright luxuriance of fresh green leaves, she caught sight of Reşit. For a time, neither moved. They just looked at each other. Then, seized by a sudden thirst, Reşit forgot how tired he was.

'A little water,' he said.

He waited beside the floral curtains where their eyes had danced. Then he heard the door creaking, and footsteps, and a few bees buzzing, and the dogs of the village barking in the distance. Thinking that every sound he heard was obscured by the next, he tried to burrow underneath them all. He dropped down against the courtyard wall, pressed his ear against the door, and took a deep breath.

'What's your name?' he said to the girl when she came outside.

'Güldeben,' said the girl. 'Don't you recognise me, Reşit?'

Reşit looked at her blankly.

'To those we have lost,' he mumbled as he gave her back the glass.

The girl giggled, then dashed back into the yard and out of sight. But her long raven hair tossed in Reşit's memory like a horse's mane.

'If only,' said Reşit to himself, 'if only . . .'

31

The sun had set and the streetlights were glowing in the half-light of evening. The hum of traffic filtered in from outside, with the clatter of closing shutters. As one after the other came rolling down, it seemed as if the entire city was closing. And perhaps this was why, as the night encroached, I kept an anxious eye on the world outside the door.

In the distance I could hear street vendors hoarsely hawking their wares; the aroma of grilled meatballs and sheep intestines swirled over the tops of dilapidated cars passing beneath electricity poles. Now and again a shadow would slip down the pavement across the way, carrying packages or nylon bags in its hands; on the balconies hanging over the street, I could see blinking lights. And then I saw a shadow with a sparkling stick across its shoulder which, as it darted fearfully through the traffic, kept changing size. It came running towards the shop.

'I was worried that the shop would be closed by now,' it said, out of breath. 'But I was wrong. Thank goodness it's still open.'

It fixed its little eyes on the door, trying to see in.

'Has the barber left?'

'Yes.'

'Where is he, then?'

'If I told you, you wouldn't believe me,' I said gravely. His eyes lit up in anticipation.

'Go on then. Tell me.'

'This morning he sent his apprentice off to get razor blades.'

'And?'

'His apprentice never came back. We waited a long time, but he never turned up.'

'And?'

'The barber lost patience and went out to look for him. But he hasn't come back either.'

He was angry. I could tell from the way he now stared at me, through narrowed, twitching eyes.

But when he spoke, there was fear in his voice. 'You mean he's lost?'

'I don't know,' I replied.

Then we fell silent, retreating into the loneliness we now shared, as the aroma of grilled meat drifted between us.

'I have to go,' said the shadow. 'If the barber returns, tell him I called.'

'Who should I say called?' I asked. But the shadow had already crossed the road and was fast disappearing.

'Say Reşit called,' it said. 'We're from the same village. He'll understand!'

32

The barber was the last person to hear the watch-man speak.

A few weeks earlier, during a mid-afternoon shave, the barber had said, 'You seem troubled,' as though he could see into the watchman's soul; as he peeled off the towel around his neck, he'd also mentioned how long the muhtar had been gone. The barber went on to say that he saw no reason for worry, for there was sure to be a good reason. Most probably the muhtar had been detained by business. He'd turn up at the moment people least expected him.

These words weren't very reassuring, of course, and the watchman gazed deep into the mirror for some time, before leaving the barber's shop in silence.

From that day on, he spoke to no one. He blew around the streets like a dry leaf. He wandered the fields while they were being planted. He lay down in the wheat for hours on end, gazing up at the sky. He was a bird among birds then, a cloud among clouds, wandering the endless blue without a thought crossing his mind – not for years. Not for aeons. Others saw him fall to his knees beside the orchard, to watch the ants all day. But he greeted no one. Nor would he acknowledge anyone who greeted him.

He sometimes walked out to the mill; he'd climb on to a willow branch and perch there like a bird, staring at the pale road that wound up to the cliffs. If he saw a shadow the size of a bird in the far distance, he'd rejoice, of course. His eyes would light up, as he thought it must be the muhtar coming home. But soon the distant shadows turned into wood-bearing donkeys, flicking their tails and pricking up their ears as they neared the village. A few flies followed, and the woodcutters with their shining axes . . . Yet the watchman stayed in the willow tree, oblivious even of the midges. And there he remained, for days on end, staring mournfully at the road. Haunted though he was by a thousand doubts, he stayed in his perch, waiting for the muhtar to come home.

Then one day, looking as miserable as a soldier in the cloak the muhtar had given him many years earlier, he walked up to the cliffs past the cabin where Fatma of the Mirrors had once lived; and from there he continued onwards under the angry noontime sun, to find lost valleys, perhaps, or lost villages, and lost cities. A few days later, when he came trailing back with the goatherds, he was still empty-handed. His face was empty, too, like his mouth, his eyes, and his heart. He wafted from street to street like an empty sack, blown from one wall to the next. He seemed to be shrinking as he went: leaving crumbs of himself on the roads and plains and cliffs and nights he left in his wake.

But still, inside that crumbling watchman, there were hundreds of other watchmen, each very different from the next. One watchman found the energy to search for the muhtar from time to time. One decided to talk again to the barber and tell him everything. One wanted to gather up his things and leave the village. One had a good, long cry. One stood puzzled inside the strange smell in the village square, wondering what to do. One even allowed himself to dream of Hacer from time to time, even though he knew this was wrong. The watchman couldn't decide which of these fellows he liked most or which ones he had been most often. Until, one day, when he thought he'd follow the one who wanted to go and tell the barber everything. Sometimes he set out to do just that, with that other watchman taking the lead, while he dawdled at the rear, passing beneath the plane tree, moving in silence towards the candle flickering in the barber-shop window. Everything around them kept quiet as they walked; kept in place, perhaps, by the night's dark clutches. Even the dogs seemed to drift into a deep sleep, and the chickens even deeper, while the birds, the children, the white-bearded old men, the doors and the windows went deeper still . . .

The watchman taking the lead walked quickly and purposefully until passing the plane tree. But then he started turning around to look doubtfully at the watchman behind him. How pleased he was when he saw that this more timid watchman was keeping pace; joy radiated from his eyes, lighting up the ground as he again pressed forward. The timid watchman followed in his glowing footsteps until they neared the barber's door. The bold watchman was close enough now to touch the window when something – a bark, perhaps, or a hacking cough – shattered the silence. Both watchmen turned around in fright, to rush off home – the real watchman first, and his homunculus fast behind.

Another watchman, who was not quite sure which one he was, darted through the courtyard gate and into the house without seeing his wife, who was at her wits' end after hours of waiting for him at the window. His wife couldn't understand him; she couldn't figure out why he would sit out in the court-yard night after night, never moving except to light a match, and no matter how she tried, she couldn't get a word out of him. Perhaps the watchman wasn't even himself any more; maybe he'd turned into a jar of lost secrets, cast into a well of silence. At his wife's desperate pleading, a few villagers came over to coax the watchman back to speech, but to no avail. The watchman would yank his cap down to his eyebrows and stare at them darkly for many long hours, before turning away to gaze into the distance. No matter where he was – at the coffeehouse, in the village square, standing at his courtyard gate or leaning against a wall – it was the mountains that tugged at him ... But his sadness gradually faded. With time he abandoned his perch in the willow tree and stopped watching the road. Instead, he returned to his post outside the muhtar's office.

Now he went there every day, to stand with his back to the flagpole and his empty eyes on the village square. He was still wearing his soldier's cloak, and sometimes he would lie down on it, cuddling his rifle like a sleeping baby. He lay there in the dead of night, and the heat of the noonday sun, watching the flag flap above him, searching in silence for the absent muhtar. Sometimes he thought he saw him in the distance, racing towards the village on horseback, and when that happened, the watchman would rush shouting into the village square. No one could understand the sounds he made, though everyone spent a long time trying to decipher them. A few people went further still; Rıza in his shop, the proprietor of the coffeehouse, and a little further down, the shoemaker – they all had their ears to the wall. But the watchman stayed all day outside the muhtar's office, and no one could be sure when he was going to shout. Sometimes the sun would set without their hearing a single cry. Sometimes the watchman would spend the whole day asleep, curled up like a mangy dog whose owner had at last returned.

One day, a few cautious villagers went over to sit with him. They didn't say a word, since they knew he wouldn't talk. Instead, without forethought, they just sat down next to him and, leaning back against the wall of the muhtar's office, they looked out at the village square. After which the white-bearded old men resting at the foot of the other wall got up as well, clicking their walking sticks as they too took their places on either side of the watchman. Next came a few youths with wispy moustaches. Soon everyone was waiting for the muhtar to come home. They were as still as if they were outside a house that had just suffered a death. They gazed emptily at the village square, seeing nothing but sadness.

The old men noticed the strange smell. Still seated, they began to search for its source. Soon they were back on their knees, forming a distinct group again, stroking their beards and conferring, searching the village square with eyes that kept vanishing into their wrinkles. Once again, they were holding a secret court. The others listened anxiously as they argued and argued about the source of the strange smell that was fast taking over the village.

Finally, the watchman could not stand it any more. He picked up his cloak and left, in such a fury that they thought he might never return.

33

This night now descending on us – it seemed to have come from another world. It had erased not just the village, but sound itself. All that was left was a bottomless abyss, and darkness without end.

And yet, though it made no difference if my eyes were open or closed, I was gripped by a strange compulsion to make some sense of my surroundings. I couldn't see a thing, or even so much as a blurry hint of a thing, but wherever I looked, I seemed to lurch in that direction, until I flinched. For a time, I tried looking around in all directions, in the hope of finding some balance. And that may be why I started trying to go deeper into the darkness. Though the leg I'd been sitting on for all this while had gone to sleep, I got back on my feet. I shuffled forward, holding out my arms to keep myself from bumping into anything. In fact, I was wrong to think my hands alone could guide me; for now I bumped into a wall, and though I tried to measure it with my hands, the way a blind man might, I was still left guessing. This might be a wall I was touching, but it seemed to have no corners: I could walk along it for months, I thought, or run for weeks, without ever finding where it ended. Or perhaps that was simply what I longed to do at that moment – to walk along that wall without a thought for where it might end – to walk just for the pleasure of walking.

But this was not to be. I was able-bodied, but also lame. I could see but I was blind. A few steps later I banged straight into a pile of bulging sacks. Sacks of chickpeas, I thought, or possibly wheat – there was no way of knowing. So I turned around, dodging the corncobs that hung from the ceiling to go back to where I'd started.

My leg was still numb. Laying it out before me like a wagon beam, I gave myself over to the rustling darkness.

Because now, from the depths, I could hear something moving – footsteps, perhaps, hiding their uncertainty as they climbed steadily upwards. I could hear breathing now, too – and this was steady enough for me to work out where the face might be, though it was something I had no desire to do.

After a few minutes had passed, I called out into the darkness, 'Is it you?'

'Yes,' said the watchman. 'It's me.'

He must be where the bags were, underneath the hanging corncobs.

'For days now, I've been longing to talk to someone,' he said, straight away. 'And in the end, I came to you . . .'

'It's good that you did,' I said. 'So tell me. What happened?'

'What didn't happen?' he said, closer. 'Is there anything that *doesn't* happen, outside these doors?'

'Well,' I said, 'I know a bit about that.'

'But I don't have a clue,' he said forcefully. 'Or rather, I can't even pull together a theory. Nothing fits. Everything in this village is getting more complicated by the minute. First things are strange, and then they get stranger . . . It's like we're cursed. Wherever I look, whatever I try to understand, I get dragged deeper into it. I can't take it any more; I just want to pack up and leave, and never come back, ever . . .'

'You shouldn't worry so much. Everything's going to be fine.'

'Wouldn't you worry, though, if you were me? As you know, the muhtar still hasn't returned. Whoever he was going to talk to about Güvercin's disappearance, he would have talked to long ago.'

'Yes,' I said, soothingly. 'He's a great man, our muhtar. If he's still not back yet, he has his reasons,

I'm sure. Perhaps his business in the city is not yet finished. He'll return the moment you least expect it.'

'He'll be surprised when he does,' sighed the watchman. 'Very surprised indeed. He still doesn't know about Ramazan. In his mind, Ramazan still lives . . . He still rides his horse, I mean; he still eats and drinks, and walks, and runs, and laughs, or – you know – pounds the keşkek before the wedding feast, and then dances the halay after . . . I've been thinking about this for some time, now: in some ways I hope the muhtar doesn't return. Because if he doesn't return, Ramazan can live on, somehow. He can spend the rest of his life dancing the halay to his heart's content in the muhtar's mind, and laughing, and pounding the keşkek. Of course, it saddens me, to think like this. I'm not being fair on the muhtar. And I know he must return, with some news of Güvercin. He has to find out that Cennet's son has come undone, and that the horse is still missing. But he never returns . . . How all this weighs down on me! Every day, Reşit comes to see me, to squawk at me like a wounded bird. Then off he goes, to search for that phantom horse for the rest of the morning and the whole afternoon, to return empty-handed each night. Then there's Cennet's son, in a world of his own, wandering the streets to show off that snake of his, and asking everyone he meets why the snow falls.

As for Rıza . . . He just sits there in his shop in a cloud of alcohol fumes, waiting to collapse in a heap, or go up in smoke, who knows which? It's not clear when he'll do himself in, or if he'll just lose it. And then, to top it all off, there's this smell . . .'

'What smell?'

'No one can figure it out. First we noticed it in the village square, then it got worse and now it's everywhere. It's such a strange smell. It smells like anything and everything, but most of all rotting meat. But I haven't told anyone that, and I'm not going to. I'm afraid to. If I do, I'm frightened someone might say the wrong thing – say it's coming from where Ramazan died. And that would be the last straw for Rıza. He'd pick up his gun and shoot whoever said it! I mean, we're on the brink of disaster, I'm telling you. And Hacer. Above all, Hacer. If they started saying that the smell came from the place where Ramazan died, she'd be out in the village square, sniffing, searching for her son! It would spell the end for her. It would kill her!'

The watchman stopped. To slip down to the floor, I thought. To rest against the sacks.

'Sometimes I ask myself why the muhtar hasn't returned, and I have all sorts of theories,' he said, dropping his voice. 'I get some very strange ideas.'

'Like what?'

'I tell myself that if the muhtar hasn't come back after all this time, he's not going to come back . . . If Güvercin is still missing, too, couldn't it have been the muhtar who kidnapped her?'

'That's absurd!'

'Why is it so absurd? He had his eyes on that girl. He was just waiting for his chance. Then one night he saw his opening, and took the girl off to some faraway village, or else, who knows, left her in a field and came back. Then he made a fuss as though he knew nothing about it: looked everywhere, got everything searched, pretended to be upset. And then, he says he's going off to the city to let them know, but instead he goes back to the girl . . . Couldn't that be it?'

'Don't say that,' I said, raising my voice. 'Don't talk nonsense for the sake of it! You don't know what you're saying!'

'No, I don't,' he murmured through the darkness. 'If only I did . . .'

I heard him stand up.

'Are you off already?'

'I'm off,' he said. 'Goodbye.'

After walking a few paces he stopped. From the way his coat rustled I guessed he was under the corn-cobs. He might even have turned his head, to look at me in tears.

'For some reason my feet are bringing me back,' he mumbled.

'That means you haven't finished what you were going to say,' I said carefully. 'Maybe you didn't get around to mentioning the thing you came to talk to me about?'

'You're right, I didn't.'

Neither of us spoke, as a great silence descended, swimming with anxious questions. Then one by one the corncobs crumbled, and suddenly there were a thousand golden raindrops speeding through the night, or that at least was what I could, or could not, see . . . While with my right hand I took hold of the leg that was now only just a little numb, waiting for the watchman to tell me what he'd come to tell me. But for some reason, he still couldn't speak, as if the words he wanted to say were locked away somewhere. And perhaps, once upon a time, the muhtar had done just this, while standing at the window, gazing into the village square: perhaps he too had tried to wrest himself free of the walls that locked him, arms and legs flailing, but still unseen.

'Are you there?' I called out after a time.

'I'm here,' he said.

'Do you have something to tell me?'

He didn't.

'I can't keep this to myself, Musa,' he said, hours later. 'Ramazan was my son!'

34

The watchman was standing outside the muhtar's office, keeping a close eye on the crowd of villagers gathered in front of him, though when he thought no one was looking, he glanced over at the road that led to the mill. He had no idea why these people congregated under the flagpole every day. That huddle of white-bearded old men – they were probably whispering to each other about the smell. They were so keen to find the source of that smell that they'd dropped everything else to come here and sit in the middle of it. Unless they had each decided separately to come and wait for the muhtar. As if to ensure that, if he did return, the muhtar would see them standing there, as he rode his horse down the mill road, now golden from wheat stalks dropped from the carts. He'd been away so long, he might even have found Güvercin, with her tresses swaying around her waist . . .

'What's that?' shouted the watchman.

At the sound of his voice, the villagers jumped up. Shielding their eyes, they looked over at the windmill. Far, far away, at the end of the golden gleam, was a crooked shadow, which moved as if gliding on water, shivering down to the stream. When it came up, it had grown. It was probably tired, because it was moving very slowly, and every few steps, it stumbled.

'Who could it be?' said Nuri.

'No one we know walks like that,' murmured the watchman. 'It has something on its back!'

'Could it be Reşit?' asked someone.

'No,' said another. 'He came back a while earlier.'

The watchman's temper flared.

'Shut up, you!' he cried.

They shut up . . . As they exchanged timid looks, a deep silence fell over the village square – deeper than the stench was wide. The silhouette was closer now and had grown even larger. It made an odd impression, as if with each new step it grew more limbs. Or perhaps it was preparing to take off into the air. As it wended its way down the golden road it slowly came to resemble Cennet's son. On his back was what looked to be a sack so large that he could only just manage to carry it.

'The madman must have caught all the snakes on the mountain,' murmured Nuri.

The crowd calmed down somewhat on hearing these words. Some were preparing to take their seats again when suddenly the watchman went racing off, his coat flapping behind him. A number of others jumped up to follow him. Cennet's son stopped when he saw them running towards him, to give them a ghastly smile.

'I fouuuuuund Güvercin!' he shouted. 'I fouuuund Güvercinnnn!'

The watchman stopped short and aimed his rifle at him. Through gritted teeth, he said, 'You filthy dog!'

Taken by surprise, Cennet's son turned to the villagers behind the watchman, as if to ask for their help. Then, with great care, he set the girl down. Moving a few paces away from her, he looked around him in alarm.

'Don't run,' shouted the watchman. 'If you try to escape, I'll shoot!'

Cennet's son made no effort to run away. His ghastly smile was now tinged with fear. As his hands were secured with a dung-caked rope of unknown provenance, and his face hit with wads of spit, he said nothing. The watchman wound the other end of the rope around his wrist and pulled him in front of the crowd. Cennet's son looked defeated, but as he scrabbled along on his knees, kicking up a cloud of dust, he lifted his eyes from time to time to stare at that soldier's cloak, and smile, very strangely. He seemed to be mocking them from a great distance: he barely noticed the stones that grazed his face, the muddy dust in his ears or the feet swarming past him on either side. Every now and then, he would still raise his head and look for Güvercin; she was a long way behind, on one of the villagers' backs. Her arms were as slender as oleaster branches. They kept vanishing, only to appear a moment later.

When they reached the village square, the watchman led his captive towards the muhtar's office. The crowd suddenly multiplied; the women who had been peering over their courtyard walls came running out, with the men who had been watching from their rooftops. The barns and threshing floors emptied. The children followed, trailed by the dogs. The women and children pushed to the front to form a circle around Güvercin, now lying on the ground. One unfastened her apron to place on the girl's bare shoulders, another used her headband to cover her hair, another smoothed down her dress and placed her bloodstained feet inside it. Their compassion provoked them to action, yet Güvercin made no response, as if she couldn't feel their warm hands, or the soft words in her ear, or their looks of concern. Instead, she curled up like a frightened hedgehog.

When Reşit and his wife came running in, the watchman tied the rope to the flagpole and looked at Cennet's son, unsure of what to do next. Reşit had his hands around his wife, who was wailing and beating her chest, and so he did not even see his daughter at first. He'd not put his cap on properly, and it rolled off as he moved through the crowd of women. Suddenly, the women took his wife by the hand and pulled her to Güvercin's side. Mother and daughter clung to each other, sobbing, and there they stood for a very long time as the crowd surrounding them continued its lament. After a while, the mother asked her daughter what had happened to her, but when Güvercin opened her mouth, not a word came out of it. Instead she stopped crying, to fall into a silence that seemed all the deeper amidst so many shrieks and shouts and wails.

Cennet's son, meanwhile, was still tied to the flagpole, and gurgling like a dog. He couldn't understand what had happened, and hadn't understood from the start. He tried to tell them where he'd found Güvercin, but tripped over his tongue. No one was listening anyway; they all passed him by. Wherever they wandered, wherever they stopped, they never deigned to look him in the eye. Now even the children he had performed for in the streets were losing interest in him, and wandering off into the crowd.

Soon they would decide to leave all this to the adults, and return to their own world.

And then Rıza came running in from wherever he had been. The sound of his rakı-flavoured voice sent a ripple of apprehension through the crowd. Fearing that he might be intending to wring the boy's neck, the watchman moved a few steps closer to Cennet's son, but what Rıza did first was to rush towards Güvercin, letting out great growls as he weaved his way between the women and children, uncertain where to rest his swollen eyes. Finally he fell to his knees in front of Güvercin, asking her who had kidnapped her, and where this man had taken her, and what they had done to her. But still the girl would not talk. Lowering her eyes to the ground, she held her breath. Rıza sat down too for a while, asking with his eyes. He might have lingered, but a moment arrived when he could no longer stand it. With a speed that seemed almost to crack open Güvercin's silence, he rose and drew his pistol. The village square began to hum. The crowd bubbled with fear. The women jumped in front of Güvercin, quickly hiding her from sight. Rıza broke his hand free of the few old men trying to stop him, and ignored the entreaties of the crowd as he made his way to the flagpole.

'Stay there!' shouted the watchman. 'If you take another step, I'll shoot you.'

Rıza stopped. The two men glared at each other.

'Hand this pimp over to me,' he said, his voice trembling with anger. 'It's high time I drank his blood!'

The watchman didn't move a muscle. He wasn't sure now if he could shoot the man who had fed and raised Ramazan all these years. As he lifted his rifle to aim, his hands began to shake.

'Get out of my sight,' he said, speaking more softly than before. 'Until the muhtar gets back, I shall answer for Cennet's son. I'm handing him over to no one!'

Rıza didn't go, of course. Despite the pleadings of the white-bearded old men, he just stood there clutching his pistol, stubborn as a goat. Reşit, caught between Rıza and Güvercin, had no idea how to calm things down. Muttering to himself, he would head straight for the watchman, only to race off to join the old men. Eventually, the imam persuaded Rıza to put his gun away. But even as he was taken off home, staggering as if he'd drunk all the alcohol in the world, he jumped into the air from time to time to announce that, sooner or later, there would be bullets raining down on Cennet's son. The watchman did not bother to respond. He seemed immune to Cennet's son's vows and curses. The watchman just stood there watching his back, until, like a bouncing ball, he vanished from sight.

'The show is over,' he said to the crowd. 'Time to go home!' The women left first, linking arms with Güvercin as gently as if they feared she might break. Then the men wandered downhill in groups of four or five, crossing the village square to fade into the shadows.

The imam had long since resigned himself to the prospect of no one coming to pray that night. When he went up the minaret to recite the evening call to prayer, there was hardly anyone left in front of the muhtar's office.

'Why are you still here?' asked the watchman.

Reşit shrugged and wandered off. He was as worried as the watchman, and as hopeless, and though he didn't know what to say, he kept glancing at the base of the flagpole. The watchman waited for a while to see if Reşit would lose his temper like Rıza and try to attack Cennet's son, but as soon as he was sure this was not his aim, he came out to sit on the doorstep.

'What'll happen now?' asked the watchman.

'If only I knew,' said Reşit. 'If only I knew . . .'

The watchman lit a cigarette, and for a moment it illuminated his whole face, but after that the only light that remained was in his eyes, which twinkled like a pair of stars. Then Reşit came over and leant against the wall next to him. They stayed like that for hours, without saying a word, listening disconsolately to the rustling of the plane tree in the village square.

'Let's marry these two off,' whispered the watchman. 'Cleanse the scoundrel of his crime. What do you say?'

'I don't know,' said Reşit.

Taking hope from the fact that this was not an absolute no, the watchman ambled over to Cennet's son.

'How about you?'

Cennet's son looked up blankly. 'Why would I marry her? I wasn't the one who kidnapped her!'

'Shut up, you scoundrel,' shouted the watchman. 'Don't lie to us!'

'I didn't,' insisted Cennet's son. 'I was on the mountains looking for my snake's aunt . . . I looked around and saw Güvercin crying in a grove of juniper bushes, so I brought her back.'

'Tell the truth or I'll pull the trigger!'

'I *am* telling the truth! She was there, in the juniper bushes! She was crying . . . Shedding huge tears, there in the darkness . . . Wasn't it the right thing to sling her on my back and bring her in? Should I have left her there?'

Perplexed, the watchman glanced up at the road from the mill, but not to look for the muhtar, for even if he had come galloping in on his horse, he could not have seen him. The night was thick and black as tar. And yet, once he had sent Reşit off and returned to his steps, his thoughts went back to the muhtar. It made him angry to think how he had simply locked the office door and taken the key with him. If he hadn't, the watchman could just open the door and lock Cennet's son inside now, and go home without having to worry about Rıza. As it was, he would be stuck here all night, shivering in the cold like a dog.

'How I wish you'd come back,' he murmured. His eyelids dropped as he slumped down against the door.

And then it seemed as if the muhtar had returned long ago, and was inside, chain-smoking at his desk and telling the watchman how to save Cennet's son from Rıza's wrath. 'We all live in several places,' he kept saying, in a voice that, with every word, lessened the watchman's despair. 'And that,' the muhtar continued, 'means that we are well placed to keep Cennet's son out of Rıza's sight. This much is clear: we must act before we have a new disaster on our hands.' The watchman propped his elbows on the desk, looking into the muhtar's eyes. 'Maybe Rıza needs to be locked up somewhere,' said the muhtar, forgetting Cennet's son outside tied to the flagpole. The watchman wondered if he was getting forgetful, if this was why he had only just returned from the city.

The muhtar must be tired. He was bumping up and down on his chair, as if he were still riding a horse, and his eyes danced with mountains, plains, highlands and green valleys cushioned in darkness . . .

The watchman's eyes shot open. So that was it – the muhtar was inside! He was more certain of this than if he'd seen him in the flesh. He couldn't help placing an ear to the door to try to listen in. He heard breathing so deep it resembled the noise from a pair of old bellows. The muhtar was inside! He pressed his ear against the door and closed his eyes tight. It sounded like the muhtar was angry, as if his face, like his breathing, was black with rage. If he was shouting, he was shouting nonsense. If he was walking, he was pacing the room, his hands clenched behind his back – raging, no doubt, at how useless the watchman had been at handling things in his absence. Why hadn't he assembled the villagers and sent them off at once to hunt the horse that had trampled that fine young man? Why hadn't he investigated that smell in the village square? 'Or if these feats were beyond you,' he imagined the muhtar saying, 'you could at least have brought Cennet's son back to his senses, and rescued your conscience into the bargain.' The watchman stood up, as if to leave the muhtar's office. Grabbing his rifle, he marched towards the flagpole.

'You're going to be out of my hands soon, you dog,' he shouted, loud enough to be heard inside the muhtar's office. 'I'm going to shoot you before Rıza does!'

Cennet's son said nothing.

'Do you hear me?' continued the watchman. 'If you don't marry Güvercin to set things straight, I'm going to shoot you before Rıza does!'

Once again, Cennet's son chose not to reply. He didn't even look up as the watchman approached. He just lay there.

The watchman leant over to look at him. His eyes were closed. In their place only eyelashes. He looked as peaceful as a baby.

'How amazing,' he said to himself. 'He's fast asleep . . .'

35

Late into the night, I decided that it would be foolish to stay in the barber's shop any longer, so I rose from my chair. My leg had fallen asleep, but like Musa Dede I felt my way across the room so as not to bump into anything. Knowing that I'd not be able to lock the door behind me, I decided I should leave the light on, so I now tried to locate the switch.

I needed to get something to eat before I went home. I imagined myself squeezing a lemon over a bowl of tripe soup, or downing a few glasses of tea. I was insanely hungry, and if I couldn't find any soup or tea, I'd pick the sesame seeds off a simit and wolf it down. Maybe I'd find a lovely little early-morning coffeehouse, with tables covered in chequered oilcloth, and flowerbeds, and a tiny pond, and a tinier fountain. Sitting down in the cool night, I would drink one warm glass of tea after the other, savouring each mouthful as the stars sparkled overhead. Then I would light up a cigarette. Other men would join me, crossing the garden like somnambulists, each to his own table, to sleep sitting up.

After groping the walls for some time, I found the light switch. I hesitated before switching on the light; I had a feeling that when it came on I might find myself somewhere completely different. In the end, I flicked the switch and gave the shop a full inspection. Everything was in its place: I need not worry that the barber would find anything missing. I thought I might come back to the shop one last time after my tea, or my soup, just to check.

At the same time, I felt guilty about abandoning my post – though my job now was not to protect the shop as much as myself. Of course, this is something I went through every month, whenever I went for a shave . . . I would hang on for hours, saying I was looking after the shop, when really I was standing next to myself, acting as my own guard . . .

No doubt I'd be back in a few hours to take a look, not at the shop, but at myself . . .

36

The next morning, the villagers forgot about their fields and workshops and crowded under the plane tree instead. Viewed from the muhtar's office, they formed a faint and blurry line: they seemed to be wavering, or even – strangely – waving, from a very great distance. Along the line, there were a number of beards, a few scattered hats, flying headscarves, hanging arms and sunken shoulders. There were eyes as well. Most of all, there were eyes . . . The blurry line became a single dark mass, keeping their limbs still and speaking only with their eyes as they closed in on the muhtar's office.

The watchman could not understand how they could close that distance without moving. For a moment, he wondered whether the rifle resting on his lap would be enough to stop the surge. During the night he had gone over to Cennet's son, who had come as close to him as the rope would allow, begging for help with those huge, frightened eyes. It was clear he'd sensed danger. He'd waited on his knees in silence, making himself small. The watchman had released his legs, and moved back, ready to strike, fearless as a general.

The grim-faced villagers were now ten or fifteen paces from the muhtar's office. Then, with a sudden jolt, they stopped . . . It was as though the watchman was keeping them at bay with his eyes alone; they couldn't pass. All their eyes were fixed on Cennet's son, there at the foot of the flagpole. In dozens – no, hundreds – of eyes, Cennet's son slowly lifted his head to face them, petrified. They shared his fear: he could see it reflected in their eyes . . . Or maybe he saw nothing in those eyes. Maybe they saw nothing in his. All they saw was fear; Cennet's son, with his hands tied, was engulfed in terror without end . . .

There was also that smell – that all-encompassing, endlessly echoing smell. And there was the watchman, stranded in its epicentre. He was loath to stay put. He still hadn't decided what to do. If he could stall the crowd just a little bit longer, then everything, he thought, would turn out all right. Maybe in that time he'd hear a horse galloping in, bringing the muhtar from afar; seeing that the villagers had taken leave of their senses, he'd intervene then and there. He'd do what he had done on the night Cennet's son was beaten: he'd give them a hard look and ask what they wanted. The villagers would say nothing, of course, and they would disperse in silence and go back to their homes. But at this precise moment, they were all moving towards him: the men and the women, the whitebeards and the foal-eyed children. Nothing about them said they had in mind to turn around and leave. On the contrary, they seemed to have taken another few paces without the watchman noticing, as they continued their surreptitious advance.

'No one move!' he shouted. 'I'll shoot, sparing no one!'

The crowd stepped back in fear. For a moment the watchman didn't recognise himself. When he shouted, it seemed as if the muhtar were shouting through him.

'Did you know Güvercin was pregnant?' asked a woman from the back of the crowd.

'I didn't,' said the watchman.

'You know now. Our girl is pregnant!'

Alarmed, the watchman jumped, without seeming to move. Or he ran, without using his limbs. He switched his rifle from one hand to the other. A wave of fatigue passed through him. He started sweating. Keeping still, and without changing his expression, he glared at Cennet's son. 'How inconvenient,' he thought, 'to be stuck here, within easy reach of anyone.' When Rıza found out that his niece was pregnant, he'd be running up there, waving his pistol, and this time no one would stop him: everyone would think him entirely within his rights. And perhaps, when a weeping Rıza shot Cennet's son in front of the whole village, he would somehow, at the same time, be shooting the horse that killed Ramazan as well . . . And then he would return in silence to his shop, and slip behind the counter, to drown himself in rakı.

Still trying to keep the crowd in his sights, the watchman glanced over at the muhtar's office. Once again he blamed the muhtar for having locked the door and pocketed the key when he set off to the city – just the memory of that moment stoked his rage. He had no choice now but to break the lock and shove Cennet's son inside. But while he did this, he needed someone else to keep the villagers at bay: given half a chance, they'd be all over him. Any of the young men below might launch the attack. If one did so much as to toss a tiny pebble – well, that alone would suffice: the others would pile in after him. The crowd would surge forward like a pack of slavering dogs . . . Leaving Cennet's son with no chance of escape. Before he found a way to undo the rope, they would tear him apart.

As his doubts grew, the watchman looked out over the crowd; they were no longer moving, not even to flick off the flies. They seemed to be holding their breath, as if they were in a dream they could hardly believe was fast approaching its climax. Or perhaps they, too, had lost their minds: for when he looked into their silent faces, he could almost see Cennet's son. The watchman didn't like this at all. Somehow he would have to have his gun barrel pointed at them while he was breaking the lock. He considered untying Cennet's son and giving him the rifle, but he soon dismissed the thought. To co-operate with a madman would be lunacy.

'The best thing would be to get one of the villagers to help me,' he thought. 'But who?'

He inspected them one by one, searching for a pair of calm and reassuring eyes. Then he spotted the barber. He was standing near the children, looking on serenely.

'Come over here,' said the watchman. 'Break this lock!'

The barber hesitated, as all eyes turned on him.

'Don't waste time. Get a rock and break this lock!'

The barber's executioner eyes sparkled as he moved through the mass of children, flying head-scarves, shivering beards, and hats, and hands, and feet. Soon he had left their fear and anger far behind.

Having found a stone the size of a fist, he strode to the door. He fell smartly to his knees and started banging the lock, as if he'd known a long time that this duty would fall to him. With every blow the glint in his eyes burned brighter. When at last the lock went crashing to the ground, the crowd began to rumble like a cloud.

The watchman untied Cennet's son and led him carefully from the flagpole to the door. The villagers moved forward several paces, as though tied to the other end of the rope.

'No one make a move,' yelled the watchman. He stood on the doorstep, reeling Cennet's son in like a dead fish on a hook. When he'd pulled his charge as far as the door, the watchman pushed at it with his elbow. The door creaked open, releasing a strong scent of rotting meat . . . All those advancing towards the muhtar's office stopped at that moment: the old, the young, the children, and even the fresh breeze blowing from the plane tree, the swallow song piercing through it, and the music of the heavens. Dropping his rope, the watchman looked at Cennet's son in shock; for inside the muhtar's office was the muhtar.

37

L eaving the barber shop, I walked towards the early-morning coffeehouse I had imagined but never seen.

The brightly lit street I'd been watching since morning was now quiet as a dead snake; before me I saw many hundreds of shuttered shops, and windows with drawn curtains, and balconies bathed in darkness. It felt like this street had been lost for hundreds of years, having shed the usual noises of a city for a moment's reflection on its past. It might still be bound to that city; it ached for release.

In the middle of an unknown road, I came to a halt. 'I've just walked down an avenue from a lost city,' I thought. 'What, then, to make of the barber shop?' Recalling its strange customers, and the apprentice, sent off to buy razor blades, never to return, and the barber who had himself gone off, never to return,

I concluded that they must all be connected in some way to this avenue. I wondered if I had been the sole witness of a great harnessing of recollections, in this barber shop in the avenue of a lost city: while I was watching the apprentice's movements, talking with the barber, arguing with the foam-faced man about his dream and looking at the picture of the dove above the mirror, I had, without knowing, been wandering amongst the fragments of its memory. It no longer surprised me that everyone who'd left the shop had got lost, or that the shop now stood empty, but even so, I wondered if they expected it to be empty when they returned. It could be that the avenue itself was not here in this world, but lost in its past, with all that I had witnessed in the barber's shop today belonging to the realm of memory. The barber I had seen today – the man I believed to have shaved me once a month for as long as I could remember – was now wandering with his apprentice through the shop's history. But the customers, the brushes, the scissors, the cologne bottles, the water-heater and the mirror – they must all be the same . . . Given the argument he'd had with me over what was real and what he'd seen in a dream, it was possible that the man with the soap-lathered face had not entered the shop with the others. Each and every customer could be from another day, or another time. But in the memory of the avenue, they were all remembered together, lined up in a row to be shaved one by one.

Stopping at a corner, I asked myself, 'Why not?' But then, as I continued on my way, I was again plagued by questions. Soon I was turning into another dark street, which led me, in time, to another avenue.

In the distance I could see a rickety old rubbish truck, chugging from bin to bin, followed by a handful of workmen. I had almost caught up with them when, without warning, they disappeared. This did not surprise me. For the rubbish trucks wandering through the night had always looked to me like ghost ships. I often followed their movements from the third floor of my apartment on Karadüş Caddesi, the street of dark dreams: I would set down my pen and watch for hours as they puttered from one street to the next. They seemed almost to sail through the darkness.

Reaching the spot where the truck had disappeared, I couldn't help but notice that it stank like the village square: just to walk through it, I had to cover up my nose. And I wondered if I, too, might disappear tonight, just as that rubbish truck had.

Unless I had already disappeared, a long time ago.

38

The barber released the muhtar from the noose.

Seeing his elongated neck, and his lolling tongue, and staring eyes, the watchman had collapsed in the doorway. And there he had lain, silent, still, and unseeing, until a few of the villagers had gathered forces to carry him out to the flagpole.

Meanwhile, the barber, Cıngıl Nuri and Reşit were looking down at the muhtar, who was lying at their feet. No one could say how long he had been there in his office. Judging by his tongue, his swollen body, and the grazes on his neck, he must have been hanging there for some time. But apart from the barber, no one was thinking at all right then. The others were pushing their way in, to stare in silence, like the villagers now swarming around the doors and windows . . . They all seemed to have forgotten how angry they were at Cennet's son. Though he had chosen to sit down next to the door, his wrists still bound, no one saw him.

As the villagers lifted the muhtar on to a carpet and carried him off, the watchman remembered to put Cennet's son in the muhtar's office and padlock the door. He didn't know if this was necessary, or even if it was really what he was doing. He might have been a sleepwalker, his body bending, and his arms and legs moving, as if answering a higher power. And when the task was done, the watchman saw himself rushing headlong across the village square, peering over court-yard walls as he went. When he arrived at the muhtar's house, he found the rest of the village already assem-bled there. They had filled the courtyard to bursting, while others looked on from the rooftops. Even the dogs had arrived, threading through the crowd, pant-ing as they absorbed the silence. There was no silence, though, at the heart of that crowd. From those standing around the reeking body came a low hum, in response to the wails of anguish coming from the house. The muhtar's wife was inside; although they had told her not to look at her husband, she had insisted. On seeing that he'd become a purple, worm-riddled lump of meat, she'd fainted. They were pouring jugs of water on her now, opening her clenched mouth with the handle of a wooden spoon, crushing garlic under her nose and slapping her wet cheeks.

Suddenly, the woman came to her senses, but when she heard that the imam did not want to wash her husband's body, she fainted again, as though the muhtar had died a second time. The imam was still out in the courtyard at this point; in a wan, ingratiating voice he was trying to explain to those around him that he could never wash the body of a suicide, as religion did not permit it. In his opinion, the muhtar was now in hell; however much good he had done in this world, he had condemned himself to this fate after taking his own life.

By noon, the muhtar was in his coffin. Fitting his great body into that narrow container was no mean feat. It seemed as though he could hear everything around him, and was still fighting for his life: perhaps he didn't really want to leave the village he had run for all these years. And his tongue – it hung down like a bulrush, reaching almost as far as his belly, refusing to go back into his mouth. Every time they tried, it would shoot out again like a purple snake. In the end they had to give up, and so it was that the muhtar entered the earth sticking his tongue out at those he was leaving behind.

Over the next few days, the village struggled to make sense of this. Theories abounded. Some said that he was sticking his tongue out at the imam, for refusing to wash his body or perform funeral rites. Others thought this claim ridiculous, and not in keeping with the muhtar they had known. He wasn't that silly – dead or not, he still knew how to behave. Even, indeed, if he had decided to stick out his tongue, there would have been a reason. It could well be that this reason would remain a mystery . . . That said, the reason, if it existed, must have something to do with what had happened during his trip into the city.

The watchman was of the same mind. Having locked Cennet's son inside the muhtar's office, he'd forgotten all about him, as he spiralled through the village like a dervish, trying to divine the muhtar's secret. He suspected that the muhtar had returned around the time when Reşit was rushing about madly, trying to kill the horse. Maybe he had come back by night, creeping in without a horse while the village reeled with the echoes of snapping bones. He imagined him slipping into his office like a cat. He wouldn't have lit a candle: he wouldn't even have touched the folds of the curtains, so as not to advertise his return. He would have lit a cigarette, and then another, to stop his curiosity dragging him to the window. But then, that night, before looping the rope around his neck, he wouldn't have been able to stop himself going over to the window to look out on to the village . . . Something deep inside him would have dragged him to it . . . And there, at the window, he would have contemplated the sorrows that had brought him to the brink of death.

The watchman could not begin to imagine what those sorrows could be. Maybe, he thought later, the muhtar had been insulted during his time in the city. Perhaps the doors of the State had slammed in his face, one by one. If that was what had happened, his confidence would have cracked like dried soil, and his beliefs snapped like corn stalks. And perhaps no one in that city had so much as noticed him. Perhaps they had made him wait days on their doorsteps; refusing to listen to a thing he said, failing to understand a thing they heard . . . Then, one day, they might have tired of him standing in their way. They might have taken him inside; forced him down long corridors into a room as big as the village. 'Güvercin the Dove, you say?' they might have said. 'Isn't that a bird?' 'No, no,' the muhtar would have replied. 'Güvercin is the most beautiful girl in the village.' 'Hmmmm,' the men might have said. 'Stay there and we'll show you what that girl's place is in the eyes of the State!' They might have chosen this moment to take down enormous books from enormous shelves, and files covered in dust, to rifle through their pages, one by one. When they saw that it would take months and months to find Güvercin, they could have called other functionaries. And soon there would have been hundreds of sharp-faced men poking their bright eyes into those books and those files caked in dust, and cursing the muhtar under their breath, and throwing him dour looks from time to time, and then returning to their task, if only because it took less effort. Finally they would have located Güvercin, of course. A group of them would have rushed in, clutching files. 'Look,' they'd have said, 'here!' And the muhtar would have looked; but all he would have seen was a tiny mark that was nothing more than Güvercin's absence. Less than a dot, even: more like an empty hole the size of a louse's eye on a page that contained too many squiggles to count. Fearing now that the empty space itself might disappear, the muhtar would have collected himself as best he could. While scanning those huge shelves, he would have tried to understand how much space he himself occupied in the eyes of the State. 'So tell me,' he would have said then, in a voice thick with surprise. 'Tell me – is this the extent of the space taken by the most beautiful girl in the village, in the eyes of the State?' The men would have knitted their brows. 'Beauty makes no difference here,' they would have said. 'Whoever told you the State was a man who cared about looks?'

'How true,' the muhtar would have said. 'Whoever said the State was a man?' Then they would have taken him by his arms, to drag him gasping to the door, and tossed him outside like a worn old sack . . .

Sometimes the watchman wondered if he was making it all up. Maybe what had happened was nothing like this at all . . . So instead he imagined the muhtar on a weary horse, sweating in the shadow of those enormous, arched, brass-ringed iron gates . . . and struggling for breath. He would have taken it all out of his saddlebags – all the trust placed in the gates of the State by the village, the road by the mill, the thyme-scented cliffs, other villages he had passed, the mountains he had crossed, the lost valleys in their shadow, the flocks grazing in the highlands, the white-cloaked shepherds and their pipes that made the mountains and rocks sigh with heartbreak – and mixed it together on the spot. The State, using the eyes of men, towered over them like a giant. Having surveyed the muhtar's magnificent display, it would have done no more than ruffle its moustache with a mocking smile that would reverberate like a curse on seven generations of Cennet's son's fore-fathers. The muhtar would not have known what to do next. For he would have come without his prayer beads, to end up face to face with the State. Unable to puff on a cigarette, either, he would have found himself in slow retreat from the State's wounding mockery. Until, without warning, the State would have surrounded him with men so thickset that a single squeezed pimple would have yielded a bucket of blood. It would have been clear from their expressions that these men found him stupid and resented every minute of their time he had wasted. Hence their fury; hence their haste. 'You!' they would have cried. 'You! You must not know how far down a lost girl is in the State's priorities, because if you did, you would never leave a village flying the flag of this State without a muhtar for this long. What kind of muhtar are you?' The muhtar would have just looked at them, of course . . . He would have had nothing to say. But rather than telling him to fuck off, the men would have remained planted before him, stubbornly silent. He would have gone pale. He would have mounted his horse and in deepest sorrow spurred it on. The horse would have been even more dejected than its burden. It would have plodded off down the road, as the brass rings on the mighty gates of the State shone in the sun, and the State's arches rose to the clouds. It would have been a long time before he escaped its shadows, shadows so heavy they seemed etched on the soil. The muhtar would have plodded on, head bowed . . . never knowing where he was bound; knowing only that it would be a place where he could die. Of course, he would have known that he could die anywhere, and yet he would have searched for a good place, so that his death would become one with the fine scenery around it.

'That means,' the watchman said, 'that he had a good reason to put the key in his pocket. He wanted his body to lie there for a while; he didn't want it to be found yet.'

'Unless,' he thought a while later, 'he was the one who kidnapped Güvercin?'

39

I found an open coffeehouse, but it looked nothing like the one in my daydream. It was a dark, narrow place crammed between a shop selling mineral oils and a fusty grocery store whose window was piled high with cigarette packets.

At first I thought it must be closed, but just as I was turning away, I spotted the waiter, bent over his blue-framed stove. What waters he was swimming through I could not say, but every time he dipped below the surface, he came bursting back up. Nevertheless, he turned around when I opened the door, watching me cross the room, even counting my steps, until I'd settled at a table, as if I, too, were in his dream.

I lit up a cigarette, already imagining the tea that he'd soon be pouring from the steaming pot to bring to my table. They smelled of wet dust, these tables, but they seemed to lack substance, as if – were it not for the overturned ashtrays weighing them down – they might have floated through the door, to wander the night streets.

'Tea?' asked the waiter. I nodded.

Rising drowsily, he wandered over to the radio. He played with the dial for a while, flipping from station to station. At long last he reached some decision, though he didn't seem overly pleased by it. As he plunked my glass of tea on the table, there was something about the sour look he gave me that told me it was part of a ritual he had played out many thousands of times.

He returned to his stove. When I saw him drift off again, I decided this would be my only tea. Because I could never bring myself to call on such a man, not even if this place were full to bursting with waiters racing back and forth. If it were up to me, I'd hem and haw instead – prattle on about how waiters never learned, and the customer was always right. I'd try, nonetheless, to catch their attention, but whenever I raised my hand, they'd all vanish.

Even if they weren't really there, they wouldn't see me. They'd pass by me as if I didn't exist.

Reşit laid his rifle across his knees and sat in front of the yard gate. The earthly world could not contain his grief. His heart was eaten through with anger. He felt too tired to move, but now and again he just about managed to lift up his head, to watch Rıza pacing the courtyard.

Rıza was not angry so much as at his wits' end; he would stop to growl something at Reşit, but his words were never clear, and he would soon go back to his pacing. After many days of this, he was making giant steps, and with each of those steps, the court-yard seemed to shrink. The moment arrived when it could no longer contain him; from time to time he would burst into the street to race down to the village square, faster and more menacing than an overflow-ing river. Here he would bang on the walls of the muhtar's office. For what was the point of fawning at the stable door, fretting like a turtledove? The time had come to storm the muhtar's office and shoot Cennet's son!

But Reşit, as always, was putting off the moment. He had seen with his own eyes that his daughter was pregnant, but he was unable to act. Action itself seemed to make him uncomfortable: even his own trembling disgusted him, and that was why he stayed sitting in the same place for days on end. He slept like a bird, and ate like one, too. If something near him moved, he'd cock his head to look at it, just like a bird did; his eyes pleaded for silence, silence without end. He wondered if he had lived through all this before – in the distant past, perhaps. So far, though, he had not managed to predict a thing. But neither had he been surprised, or startled, or shocked, by anything he'd seen. Such emotions seemed beyond him. But the moment he saw or heard something, it called to mind a half-forgotten dream. One by one, familiar details would command his attention. They might be blurry at first, but with time they became clearer. So that now, as far as Reşit was concerned, the only blur remaining was Güvercin's pregnancy. This could explain why he had shut her in the stable, vowing not to let her out until she identified the father!

His wife would come running out of the house. Falling to her knees, she would beg Rıza to talk her husband down, but Rıza would pay her no attention. She'd grovel around her husband's brother like a dog, for all to see, stomping around the courtyard before dragging him inside. They would fight like this several times a day, and there were other times when they raised their voices so high the whole village could hear them. The women would peer over their courtyard walls to listen in silence. Of course, they ducked whenever Rıza raised his voice, leaving behind them a row of worried ghost faces. The children were more forthright, however. They would sit in a row on the wall, like statues almost, and watch for hours, never blinking once. They might not have understood what was going on, and yet they waited there patiently, just to hear Rıza swearing. They must also have heard that Güvercin was shut in the stable, and that would have got them curious, thought of course there was no hope of taking a look for themselves. The stable door was Reşit, the walls Reşit, and the roof Reşit. There was no getting past him. No one, that is, except for the watchman.

He came by every other day, and whenever he did, Reşit would move slightly to one side, as if to let him through. At first he wasn't so accommodating, of course. Eyeing the gaggle of women behind him, he'd press his back against the stable door, rifle at the ready, impervious to their pleas. He wouldn't talk to anyone else, either. He'd just stand there grinding his teeth while the women insisted that Güvercin, being pregnant, needed their attention. The little lamb might be in pain, they'd say; she could be on the verge of death, they'd wail. Show some mercy! What the mother suffers, the child suffers in turn! In response, he'd only grind his teeth some more. Until finally, the women gave up and went home, or went in to see Güvercin's mother. With time, though, things got easier. The watchman would nudge open the stable door to enter into darkness so thick you could bounce a stone against it. The windows, which looked out on to the cherry orchard, were no larger than cows' eyes, casting a thin light on the manger and nothing else. The watchman would linger at the door, unnerved by the strong smell of horse, which took his mind to the horse that had killed Ramazan: it could be here. As his eyes became accustomed to the darkness, he'd begin to see posts and feedbags and piles of straw on the floor. He advanced, very slowly, lest he startle Güvercin.

'Listen to me, my girl,' he said in a confident voice. 'You have no reason to fear. Tell me everything that happened to you from the start . . . Tell me so we can find a solution to this problem . . . Look, it is growing in your tummy.'

Güvercin was silent.

'Who kidnapped you?'

Silence.

'Tell me, was it Cennet's son?'

No response.

'If you tell me who it was, I'll get them to marry you. I'll persuade your father, I promise!'

The girl was silent. And eventually the watchman asked her the question that had been eating away at him for a very long time.

'Or else,' he whispered, 'was it the muhtar who kidnapped you? Look, he's dead now. He hanged himself . . . There's no need to be afraid. Come on now, tell me.'

The girl said nothing. It was the same with her father, and her mother, and Hacer and Rıza: with each and every one of them, she remained stubbornly, and unfathomably, silent. Emerging from the stable, the watchman would frown. Speaking loud enough to be heard in the darkness, he would ask Reşit how to get the girl to speak. But Reşit was no better; he would answer with a shrug of his shoulders, before staring at a fixed point on the ground for hours on end.

'Shall we marry her off to Cennet's son?' asked the watchman.

'With that madman?' came Rıza's voice from the other end of the yard. 'Are we going to marry Güvercin off to that madman? Not in this world!'

'And why not?'

'What, should the girl get into bed with his snakes? And anyway, doesn't the holy law forbid getting engaged to a madman?'

At that, the watchman would fall silent. He'd plant himself in front of Rıza and stare at him wordlessly before leaving the yard. The barber would watch him come back past his shop at all hours of the day. He'd carry on watching until the barrel of his rifle vanished behind a wall. He'd catch himself smiling, but when he did, he'd turn his back on the village square and return to his shop. A wave of fatigue would come over him, as every aspect of his being – his gaze, his sense of touch, his smile and his silence – began to wane. Or unravel. Or shrink, even, as bit by bit, the flesh was torn from bone. And perhaps that was why he drew what strength he could from everything he passed: if he happened to see an earthenware jug, for example, he'd carry it in his mind for a while more. When words left his mouth, he would let them wander around like floating mines for a few days before recalling them to his ears. Or he'd delve under the veil of time to pluck a dream from the darkness, to let it play out before his eyes once again.

All this made the barber wonder if he ought to leave the village. He'd been thinking about it more and more these days – thinking back to the time he took his suitcase and came here, and wondering why. He imagined a city, and in the city a street, and in the street a shop, and in the shop he imagined a barber.

The barber must be all alone by now, as he stood by the window, looking out through narrowed eyes.

By the time I finished my tea, the coffeehouse had filled with drowsy men. I had no recollection of the door opening. I couldn't for the life of me recall seeing them come in. But here they were, sitting all around me, each with his empty glass of tea. Some were lost in thought; some were dozing with their chins on their chests. Others were resting their heads on their hands, and looking blankly at nothing in particular. Written on each face was a tale of the same burdens, the same thoughts, or even maybe, without their even knowing it, the same hearts. A few were now resting their heads on the tables, to sleep in earnest. 'Who can know why they're so tired?' I thought. 'Who could say whose weariness weighs them down?' And then, in my obstinacy, I again tried to remember when I'd seen them coming in.

'Maybe,' I said to myself, 'I, too, fell asleep a little while . . . and that's when these men came then. They crept through the door and went each to their own table and sat down. And after that, they slurped down their tea too quickly for me to notice. Then they coughed, but I didn't hear that either. Or they spoke amongst themselves as the waiter was bringing them tea. Asked for an address, for example. Conversed about work, or money, or women, without my hearing a thing. I didn't hear them looking at me, either. Just as I did not hear the silences in between their words. Or was I seeing what happened after I left? The men in the coffee-house weren't there yet, and after I left they all came in one by one, settling down at these same tables to sip these same teas until they dozed off. And then, maybe one of them would stare blankly at this empty table, and, catching a glance of someone who looked like me, they would shudder. Or was I that person? Or is that just how we are all born, with a fleeting shudder – doesn't the whole adventure begin there? I jumped up from the table, desperate now to pay for my tea and leave before I fell prey to this nonsense. But I couldn't find the waiter. I lingered there awhile, pacing back and forth, thinking he must have gone to the toilet or gone to throw out the rubbish, and would presently return. Now and again, I would peer out into the darkness, until at last one of the sleeping men lost patience.

'What are you doing, walking around like that?' he asked, as once again he rested his head between his arms.

'I can't find the waiter,' I said, impatiently. 'I was going to pay for my tea.'

But already, the man was drifting off to sleep.

'Leave the money on the counter,' he mumbled.

'How much does a tea cost?'

'Leave as much as you want, what difference does it make?'

42

Knowing that her son had been allowed to go hungry for days on end, Cennet would bring a few sheets of yufka and a bowl of yoghurt to the muhtar's office every morning. Every morning, she'd whip across the village square like a whirlwind, so fast and furiously that it seemed her own body might come undone. Planting herself at the door, she would wait for the watchman to come outside, and after he did, she would plead with him for hours on end, crying her eyes out, and even grabbing his legs and begging, but no matter how she implored, he wouldn't let her see her son. The watchman was at least as stubborn as Reşit, and in much the same way that Reşit had, in essence, become the stable door, the watchman had become the door of the muhtar's office. Standing firm, rifles in hand, they each served as the other's echo. Blind as doors, they were, and deaf as walls. They had both turned to stone, while their minds wandered far, far away.

'On your way, and stop yowling like a cat,' the watchman would cry. 'I'm not letting that scoundrel eat a mouthful!'

Cennet, still holding the yufka, would stop and stare.

'You still say you have a son?'

And still, she'd stare.

'You have nothing remotely resembling a son!'

And this was her cue to bow her sad head and set out for home, clutching the yufka that would soon go stale. She would turn now and then, hoping for some drop of mercy, but to no avail. With time, she began to worry that the watchman might get so fed up seeing her at the door of the muhtar's office that he'd take it out on her son, so she decided to keep her distance, and took to sitting at the foot of the plane tree instead, her bowl of yoghurt at her feet. From here, she would watch the muhtar's office for hours on end. Maybe she thought the watchman would see the bowl of yoghurt and remember how hungry her son was inside; ground down by his own stubbornness, his heart might begin to soften . . .

But the watchman's heart refused to soften. He wandered through the village like a mad cow, and when the old men tried to reason with him, even, he paid them no heed. He seemed at times to be a ghost in watchman's clothing. Still fearing Rıza's rage, he'd keep looping back to the muhtar's office, to check on Cennet's son. In fact, he hadn't even decided how long he was going to keep him there. He could fix the sentence and hold him here for the duration, or he could bind him hand and foot and cart him off to the city. Though taking him into the city didn't seem like a very good idea; he didn't think those State officials would know what to do with a madman. They would laugh at him, laugh him right out of court, saying, 'Whatever possessed you, to bring us a madman?' 'Güvercin,' the watchman would say, 'but Güvercin the Dove . . .' And the State officials would say, 'Hmmmmm.' 'What is Güvercin the Dove?' they would ask, just as they had asked the muhtar. 'Isn't that a kind of bird?' 'No, no,' the watchman would reply, just as the muhtar had done, months earlier, 'Güvercin is the most beautiful girl in our village!' Hearing that, the men would fix their eyes on him, and say, 'So. Was that the girl that this dog kidnapped?' The watchman would stammer out a yes, before adding, 'What's more, he got her pregnant!' Again the men would say, 'Hmmmm,' exchanging silent looks, exuding such fury that Cennet's son would begin to shake like a leaf, his eyes widening as he appealed to the watchman for help.

The watchman would pay him no attention, of course. Instead, he'd frown importantly. And then the men would gulp a few times, and one would say, 'That means . . . That means Güvercin is a girl?' 'Yes, a girl . . .' 'And not a bird?' 'No, not a bird . . .' 'You're absolutely sure of this – she's not a bird?' 'She's not!' But the next in line would say that she certainly sounded like a bird to him. 'And to me,' another would say. 'In fact it sounds like a novel I read months ago, and then forgot . . .' The watchman would stand there helplessly. So would Cennet's son . . . They would stand there for hours as the men argued amongst themselves as to whether or not she was a bird. Maybe days, maybe months . . . And then one would say, 'Hey! I just remembered what this was all about!' 'What was it?' they'd ask, in a chorus. 'Um, didn't a muhtar come in to see us?' the man would say. 'Didn't he tell us about a girl like that, who had disappeared?' Whereupon the men would again say, 'Hmmmmm,' as they took their minds back. 'Hmmmm,' this chorus would say. 'And didn't we show him how important this girl was in the eyes of the State?' 'Did he faint?' one would ask. 'Why?' another would reply. The first would say, 'Why would . . .' only to pause and burst into laughter. And then the others would join in. They would laugh and laugh, for days, perhaps years . . . Unable to get a word in edgewise, the watchman would give up, and take Cennet's son back to the village, bemoaning his fate with every step.

'Get up,' he said one day. 'Get up and fuck off!'

At first, Cennet's son was too shocked to move. He looked up at the watchman, expecting another beating.

'Get out of my sight!' said the watchman. 'Go to whatever hell you like!'

But Cennet's son was in no hurry. He stumbled over to his mother, who was sitting under the plane tree. Before long there was a great crowd in the village square, watching mother and son embrace. And then Cennet linked arms with her son and led him home, leaving her yoghurt bowl behind. Rıza came out of his shop to scowl at them.

'Don't stare like that,' said Cennet. 'He's half-dead already, come and take the rest!'

Rıza didn't know what to say for a moment. Then he waved his hand, as if to say 'Take him away', and went back inside. This cheered up the watchman no end. Standing at the window, he mumbled a few words. 'At last,' he said, 'you're safe. From now on, you need no longer fear Rıza's wrath . . .'

But in the days that followed, there was no way of knowing if Cennet's son was still alive. No one had seen him since he stumbled out of the muhtar's office to be taken home by his mother; no one had heard him speak, or breathe, or caught even the most fleeting glimpse of him. Everyone was curious to know, of course, but no one dared to ask. The villagers had somehow come to a silent agreement that he was not to be touched, not even by words. Instead they had to wait and see . . . If something should emerge from this silence, it would do so of its own accord. The boy was already as damaged as could be. The blows had been struck, and his bones had been broken. They had to wait and see . . . If he was back in the mountains, then they should leave him to wander as far as he liked, breathing in the scent of thyme, listening to the birds' wings flapping, and the snakes hissing, to his heart's content . . . If he wasn't in the mountains, but by his mother's side, then let him sleep like the lambs of May . . . Let him drink ayran, and scratch off his scabs, while his mother shooed off the flies that swarmed around the pus, and wailed. They had no choice but to wait and see . . .

Cennet's son was alive, and at his mother's knee. He stayed there for weeks, maybe, and at just the point when they'd almost forgotten about him, he started wandering the streets again. He had an odd way of walking, and he gave odd looks to the children dancing in his wake, and every so often he would stop to shake out an imaginary sheet and grin. This may explain why the children started calling him 'the ghost'. Soon everyone else in the village was calling him that, too. It almost seemed as if a stranger going by that name had just arrived in the village, to scare the children on the streets. Every time he gave them a scare, they would, even as they scattered, try and scare him back. But they could not ruffle him: he smiled calmly when he smiled, talked calmly when he talked. He'd assemble them in front of him and prattle on for hours. They might not understand a thing he said, but somehow he had become their teacher and commander – sometimes he would get them in line and made them put their hands on the ground, then on his order they would run to whatever point he indicated. The children would skip about like a battalion of skittish rabbits, leaving behind them a cloud of dust.

One day, the ghost picked up a snake from some-where, coiled it around his neck and started marching in front of the children. First they did a grand tour of the village, laughing together each time they stopped in front of a courtyard gate. Peals of laughter would emerge from the dust clouds, as reflections of breath-less children flashed across the windows. Birds flew out of this cloud of laughter, to scatter in all directions, like leaves. Then suddenly the village itself seemed to float away, from its streets, walls and windows, its chimneys and sounds, and in the void it had left in its wake, there was only silence. There was only the gaze. Suddenly the children came back into view again. They were following the ghost, and followed by great mountains of dust, as they marched towards the village square. And here this motley crowd of waving limbs lost momentum, and came to a halt. The ghost raised his hand, first to silence them, and then to call them to order.

'This is my belt,' he said, showing them the snake. 'Do you like it?' The children beamed, and some tittered.

'I have a question for you,' said the ghost.

They waited.

'Who sent me this belt, do you think?'

The children exchanged looks.

'Whooo?' he wailed. 'God,' said the ghost. 'God, who created the muhtar! And the watchman, and my mother, too!'

The children fell about laughing.

'Take this belt and look at it,' he said.

Planting his legs wide apart, the ghost surveyed them, and it almost seemed as if he were drawing new faces for them, and repointing their eyes, in preparation for the show. Then, taking the snake from his neck and wrapping it around his waist, he fed its tail into its mouth. The snake seemed to want to help him, for now he bit off some of its tail and even swallowed it. The ghost raised up his hands in victory. The children enjoyed it – in fact, they roared. Some jumped on their friends' shoulders, some beat their knees in laughter, while others sat down and bent over, almost hitting their heads on the ground before straightening up again. Hearing the clamour, the men came pouring out of the coffeehouse, the women from their courtyards, and the whitebeards from the wall where they'd been sunning themselves, and they all moved slowly towards the village square, to find out what was happening.

The snake that was coiled around the ghost's waist was still trying to swallow its tail. The ghost was grinding his teeth, and writhing in pain, and the more he writhed, the more the children shouted. Everything seemed to be lost in the children's screams, everything seemed to change from dust to noise and noise to dust again. Suddenly, there was a round of applause. The ghost waved his hands, to say something no one understood, as the applause grew louder. When the ghost bent over, it again grew louder, and then louder still, until the entire village square was writhing and hissing like a snake. And this was the moment when the men and women converging on the village square started running, fearing they were already too late.

Suddenly the children fell silent.

The ghost was crumpled up on the ground, a greenish liquid seeping from his mouth.

43

It had been a long time since I'd left my tea money on a table near the stove and put the coffeehouse behind me. With growing apprehension, I plunged into the darkness, determined to go straight back to the barber shop. I turned into a street, waited for a spluttering rubbish truck to struggle up the slope, spreading a foul smell, and then fluttered like a lonely moth through a neighbourhood of huge apartment blocks, to be swallowed up by a deep, dark hole that turned out to be a street lined with stairs. Still I walked on.

And the longer I walked, the more urgent it seemed to reach the barber shop before it was too late. So great was my sense of urgency that I paid little attention to the streets as I was passing through, or the stairs, or the balconies hanging over me, or the billboards submerged in darkness, or the rubbish on the pavements. All I could think about was the barber's shop. The mirror shone like a lake as I approached. The scissors sparkled and flashed as the night receded, moving ever more distant until it vanished into thin air.

I paused as I entered a wide avenue lined with palm trees. It occurred to me then that I had been passing through a neighbourhood I'd never seen before. I looked around me in fear. All I could see was humming desolation. 'I must have been daydreaming,' I said to myself. 'I must have taken a wrong turn . . .'

Then I tried to retrace my steps, running down the hill I hoped would return me to the neighbourhood of huge apartment blocks. Instead it took me to a tiny little street filled with the smell of leather. Breathlessly, I ran from one end to the other, diving into the first street on my left. This took me into another street in which the air rang with a watchman's whistle. In time it led me out to a winding cobblestone avenue. I continued along this avenue for many hours. My feet began to drag, but still I kept looking for the barber shop. I was losing hope: I didn't know what to do, or which street I should dodge into, or where I was going. It was as if a great hand were playing with my memory, or erasing all the streets of the city from the face of the earth, or taking just the avenue that was the key to all else, and moving it to some other city . . . At that moment, any or all of these things could be true, but there was no way of knowing.

I knew just one thing: either the barber shop was lost, or I was.

44

When the first snow fell over the village, Reşit was still standing in front of the stable door. Behind him was a sheepskin, and on his shoulders rested a rose-patterned quilt that reeked of rancid sweat. He was stiff as stone, and cold as the snow. From the moment he'd thrown Güvercin, punching and kicking, into the stable, he'd been living a new life. Every mealtime, cooked food was brought to the door; everything he needed – socks, tobacco, tinder, water, flint and tea – was brought to the door and left at his feet. Now and again Reşit would get up to relieve himself: he'd walk over to the left-hand corner of the courtyard, place his rifle on the pile of rotten planks, amongst the spider-webs, slip down his trousers and strain, but not for a moment did he take his eyes off the stable door.

For he feared that if he left her alone for just a moment, the villagers would rush in and take Güvercin home with them. At each hearth there would be a Güvercin, he thought, at each table another. In every half-lit closet, at the edge of each sofa and under every set of blankets, there would be a Güvercin, and Reşit wouldn't know where his daughter was or who he could take her back from. And this was why he hadn't gone to Cennet's son's funeral all those months ago. While all the other men in the village, and their wives and children, had assembled in the village square, he was in front of the stable door. When the children took the snake that had swallowed its own tail, killing both Cennet's son and itself, and mounted it on to the end of a stick, and paraded it through the streets, he was in front of the stable door. When they spoke of the boy's waist being squeezed tighter and tighter, until it was the width of an oleaster branch, he was in front of the stable door, no doubt, and when they spoke of Cennet going blind from crying, he was still there. He heard everything from the villagers as they came and went. They told him that the children had been even sadder than the adults about what had happened; that they had walked behind the coffin all the way to the cemetery. They told him all this while he sat entirely still in front of the stable door.

A few times a week he went inside to interrogate his daughter, but he had yet to get an answer. Güvercin kept her silence, as slowly it faded into the darkness of the stable. It was difficult even to see her; for her eyes had got lost in the silence, and her eyebrows in her hair, and her hair in the darkness, and the darkness in the distance. The only thing he could see was her swollen belly, and whenever Reşit opened the door, the fact of that belly resounded like a drum. The larger it grew, the more his world narrowed. He would rush for the door, taking his unanswered questions with him, but also the image of that belly, which he could not erase from his mind.

Sometimes, when elsewhere in the village they were gathering together around steaming bowls of soup, or lighting lamps one by one to bring life to the darkness, while the whitebeards at the foot of the wall headed home for bed, tapping their canes, the old women would come to Reşit. When he was still a snot-nosed child, these scrawny and toothless old biddies had always been ready with a stuffed flatbread for him, or glasses of water. They'd patted his head, wiped the sleep from his eyes with their headscarves, performed little rituals to protect him from the evil eye, and now they showed an alarming intuition in choosing the hours of the night when he was at his weakest. Reşit cried blood while listening to them. He questioned himself, and looked inside his heart, and gritted his teeth, but not for a second did he let on. He looked at these women as blankly as the walls to either side, and the door behind him. And so, when the women said, 'Let's take this girl out of the stable and put her to bed,' they were talking to a door. When they advised him not to intervene in these matters until the baby was safely born, they were talking to a wall. They got no response, of course, and many hours later, when the imam launched into his last call to prayer, they would lose hope and return home. And after their footsteps rang in the streets, they would echo in Reşit's mind until, at long last, they were lost in the darkness inside him.

Then he, too, would settle into that darkness, as he sat there smoking, and listening to the dogs barking at the other end of the village. Much later, as the night grew thicker, swallowing up the birds in their sleep, muffling the barking dogs, swamping the villagers, drowning the plains, and passing over the cliffs to spread further still, Reşit looked across the snow-covered rooftops and noticed a dark stain . . . The stain kept twitching, and jumping from roof to roof. It seemed as lithe as a black cat, but as it came closer, it burst through its silhouette. Suddenly, a pair of silver pebbles shone out from the stain, and in their light that stain took the form of a horse. Reşit rose slowly and walked towards it, watching it intently as his feet creaked and cracked through the snow. He wanted to make absolutely certain it was

287

what he thought it was before he aimed his rifle and fired . . . He looked for the wild winds in its mane, the smell of blood on its hooves and the bones crunching in its ears. But the horse refused to oblige: it stood lively on the snow, flicking its ears and breathing fire. It was still far away, or else he himself was far away. Try as he might, he couldn't judge the distance.

Yet on one night like this, as it crashed through a cloud of darkness and snow, the horse laughed at him; just like Cennet's son, he laughed at Reşit, and then he laughed some more. This laughter achieved what the old women had not, for all their nocturnal visits. It sent Reşit into a fury, and the next day he locked the stable tight and went off to find the horse again. Rifle in hand, he vanished into the mountains.

And once he was off wandering from cliff to mountain peak, the old women swarmed to the stable door. For days on end, they couldn't find a key to fit the lock, though they could see Güvercin through the gaps in the wood. As soon as she heard their voices, she came up towards them, standing among the cowpats, her face speaking her longing for a woman's warmth.

The women first asked her whether her pains had begun or not. Güvercin sobbed in response. Taking this to be a yes, the women exchanged looks, not knowing what to do next. For days, they waited in silence beneath the ice-covered eaves. They passed bowl after bowl of food through the window that was the size of a cow's eye, and that looked out on to the cherry orchard, just as her mother had done in secret, every night . . . They would rush back to their houses, in fact, and return with bowl after bowl of molasses, pickles and yoghurt. There were many different types of molasses, some made from sesames, and others made from poppies, and pickles made from unripe melons, and peppers, and tomatoes and carrots, and with one voice they told Güvercin that everything would be fine: 'For now, just eat . . .' But more than the food that came through the window she needed those who brought it; she struggled to distinguish their faces, their breathing, their voices, so that she could recognise each and every one. She could make out Hacer, for example, and her mother, and Cıngıl Nuri's wife, and the muhtar's wife, too, and though she couldn't see them, that sad, long-haired girl could recognise them all, and for a moment, she was happy.

But whatever they did, she would not tell them who had made her pregnant.

'I won't say,' she said once in response to her mother's whispers. 'I'd rather die . . .'

It was at the afternoon call to prayer, maybe; and her mother, left outside with her suspicions, was aghast at hearing these words . . . When she collected herself, she resorted to other questions, to work out when the birth would be.

Meanwhile Reşit was in the mountains, listening to the echo of a bullet he had just shot at the cliffs.

'Damn it,' he said, between clenched teeth. He put his rifle back on his shoulder and walked back to the village. A day in these mountains, and the snow had blinded him. Over and over, he had thought he'd seen the horse and aimed his rifle, but just as he was about to shoot what was no more than the ghost of a horse, he came to his senses and trudged on, shaking his head in despair.

'What was that shooting noise?' asked the watchman, standing before him in the village square.

Reşit bridled.

'I shot it.'

'You saw the horse?' asked the watchman.

'No,' said Reşit. 'For a few days there's been a bear wandering near the village. I shot at it.'

'Did you get it?'

'Not this time, but maybe the next!'

Together they walked through the evening darkness. The watchman was silent; since the muhtar's death, he'd been subdued. He rarely got upset, and he rarely got sad. He thought deeply before speaking. He'd let his moustache grow until his upper lip had vanished underneath it.

They stopped under the plane tree.

'The time has come for us all to search for that horse together,' said the watchman. 'I will let everyone know tonight. Don't set out alone tomorrow, wait for us!'

'Agreed,' said Reşit.

'Make sure you don't forget,' added Cıngıl Nuri.

Reşit hadn't seen him. He turned to find him right behind the watchman, wearing rubber boots.

'Let's all find that killer together,' said Rıza, from inside Cıngıl Nuri.

Reşit almost gasped.

'Let's find him,' he said to Rıza, or Nuri (he didn't know which).

'I'll come too,' said the barber.

But Reşit couldn't see him; he was turning in the snow, trying to find the barber in Rıza's face, in Nuri. He could hear his voice, which meant he must be in there somewhere. Maybe he had come with his apprentice.

'Why are you wandering around like that?' asked his wife.

Reşit stopped in the middle of the courtyard; he looked around blankly, trying to figure out where he was: he saw the stable door beneath the icicles, and the chicken coop, submerged in darkness, and the cart, and on the other side the wooden staircase leading up to the house, and his wife.

'You'll kill that girl soon,' said his wife, when their eyes met. 'Your daughter's in labour!'

Reşit seemed not to hear. Looking away angrily, he crossed the courtyard to race up the stairs.

'Just so that you know – the girl will give birth sometime today!'

He had planned to pause on the top step and curse his wife, but he didn't stop. He pushed through the door and dropped his rifle. Longing to lose himself in the half-light, he gave himself over to the scent of chickpeas, and of thyme, sorrow and despair. As he plunged deeper into the darkness, he kept his silence with him, and his past.

His wife, when she called up to him, seemed very far away. 'Can't you hear me, husband?'

Then Güvercin's screams rose up through the air, flapping like a pair of disembodied wings . . .

45

The day broke when it broke, yet in some godforsaken street I was still looking for the road that led to the barber's shop. I was exhausted – after many hours of walking down these dark streets, I was only now coming to recognise them, and I was beginning to stumble. Despite my urgent need to arrive at my destination as soon as humanly possible, I was slowing down, and sweating like a horse. I had, somehow, become Cennet's son. I was stepping outside the muhtar's office, to pass through a village square that looked like a city. Soon, no doubt, I would emerge from beneath the rustling plane tree with my pack of imaginary children. Turning right at the grindingstone, I would dance past the whitebeards at the foot of the wall, who would rouse themselves to watch me head for our courtyard gate.

And the moment she saw me, Cennet would say, 'Heavens. What is this?' as though I'd never died. 'Heavens, what is this...' And then she'd get up, stand right in front of me, trying to get a good look through eyes swollen from crying. And she'd murmur, 'What type of dream is this?' A shadow would pass across her face, a shadow resembling a dead snake on a stick, and in its wake, my coffin, passing through the streets, and screams, floating, and shoulders, hunching. Clutching my coffin, a row of hands, and beneath them, the villagers, trudging, trailing grief, and silence . . . Cennet would see herself in that crowd; maybe for a while she would watch herself looking at my coffin . . . If I were Cennet's son, I wouldn't leave her like that for too long. I would open up my arms and run straight into hers.

But instead I stopped: I had turned from the village square into a bright and bustling avenue. For a time, I watched the honking cars flow past, as the shutters rolled up, amid bursts of happy song. I listened to the simit and salep sellers hawking their wares.

I gave up trying to find the barber shop. I crossed the road, and plodded down the pavement, thinking I had no choice but to go home.

46

The villagers assembled at the foot of the plane tree in the early hours of the morning, without quite knowing what they were there for. They shuffled about drowsily, glancing at each other from time to time, adjusting the cartridge boxes at their waists, and listening to the snow crunch beneath their feet. Then finally they set off down the road to the mill, leaving behind the smoke curling from the chimneys of the village, the blackened rooftops and the white-bearded old men peering out from the windows of the coffeehouse.

Leading them was the watchman, who was wearing his soldier's cloak. Now and again he would turn, steam billowing from his mouth as he issued instructions to those behind him. 'Everyone spread out as far as they can,' he could be saying. 'If we all spread out we'll be able to search a larger area.'

Unless he was warning them to be careful, telling them not to go haywire when they'd spotted the horse, not to get in such a panic that they shot themselves! It could be that he was swearing at the horse, launching a jeremiad against the last seven generations of horses from its stable. It was clear he was in a rage: the clouds of steam were coming fast and furiously, and the skirts of his cloak were shaking up a storm.

Then they split up and spread out slowly in all directions until they were out of each other's range. Each trudged through the snow for many hours, driven by a vision of a horse. Each smoked one cigarette after another, each began to shiver from the cold, each narrowed his eyes to scan the horizon. Around noon, they came together again, to march across the plain and up into the mountains, like an army in retreat. Exhausted, they passed the house where Soldier Hamdi and Fatma of the Mirrors had settled their accounts, forming an enormous arc to climb the cliffs. On they went, across unknown hills, beset by wild and wayward clouds that dampened their hopes, and a fierce wind that scraped the ice off the ground and dashed it to pieces.

'This was where I saw the bear,' said Reşit.

The watchman turned around to squint at the juniper grove that Reşit was pointing to.

'Wouldn't it be hibernating?' asked the barber. Reşit shrugged. He was listening to the cliffs as though he could still hear the bullet he had lobbed at the bear the day before. Then a speckled partridge flew up in front of them, and dived back into the bushes. Everyone jumped . . . And then went still, as if to conjure up the flapping wings that had now swooped away. Afterwards they joined forces and went rushing down into the juniper grove. In their haste, they loosened a few clumps of snow from branches above them; so forlorn was their fall that the juniper bushes could not help but sigh; their sigh shook the other branches, until all through the deep green grove, there were snowflakes swirling. As the last light faded, a darkness inside the darkness stirred. No, it didn't just stir – it let out a weird moan as it moved towards the villagers.

Before anyone could make sense of this apparition, let alone be shocked by it, the barber had aimed his rifle and fired.

'That's the bear!' shouted Reşit. 'That's the bear that's been wandering around here the last few days!'

The villagers, restored to safety, peered curiously at the bear.

'Let's take this bastard to the village,' said the watchman.

As he fell to his knees to tie its back legs, he looked up at the barber.

'So,' he said. 'It turns out you're a real marksman.'

The barber blushed, and forced a smile.

Then they returned to the village, dragging the bear and a convoy of ragged clouds all the way to the muhtar's office, and leaving behind them a long, winding trail of blood on the snow. The watchman again led the way. He'd draped the rope over his shoulder and tied it around his wrist, but the going through the snow was slow. The villagers trudged behind the bear with their rifles and handguns. The barber, who had still not quite found his place in the village, despite all the years he had lived there, walked alone behind all the others. Indeed, he almost seemed to be breaking off from them altogether: though every step took him closer to the village, he seemed to be further away. And when the whitebeards, hearing the villagers return, left the warm tin stove to huddle wide-eyed around the coffeehouse window, they, too, seemed to notice; they exchanged looks, whispered, 'What's happened to that one?' Then they saw the bear and their spirits lifted, for they thought it must be the horse. Then the children descended noisily upon the village square, chased by a few of their mothers, and soon there was such a crowd that the old men could see neither bear nor barber.

The watchman was still dragging the bear, which seemed even heavier now, with all those children's eyes on it. When at last it was lying outside the muhtar's office, he tied the rope tight around the flagpole.

'Isn't it dead?' asked one of the children.

'Of course it is, son,' said the watchman. 'It died the moment the bullet hit it!'

'Soooo . . . then why are you tying it up?'

The watchman stopped in his tracks. He looked at the bear, and he thought about Cennet's son. But by now the old men had come out of the coffeehouse. Passing through the huddle of children, they came up to the bear, beards quivering.

'Who shot it?' one asked.

'The barber,' said the watchman.

The old men turned their heads in unison, searching for the barber, but they couldn't find him. In any event, they didn't have the chance. For now a boy came careening out from behind the plane tree, shouting at the top of his lungs. A roar went through the crowd.

'What's he saying?' asked the watchman.

'Güvercin's given birth!' cried the shoemaker.

At first Reşit couldn't quite understand. He seemed almost to be asleep with his eyes open. Then suddenly he pushed through the crowd, sprinting past the plane tree in a single breath. For a moment he feared for his daughter's health. Then he banished the thought, though it chased him like a dirty cloud, down one winding street to the next.

At last, Reşit rushed in through his gate. The courtyard was packed with women, who parted when they saw him to pave his way to the stable door.

'She gave birth all by herself,' said one.

He took the key from his pocket.

'She bellowed like a cow,' said another. 'Thank God they both survived!'

With shaking hands, he turned the lock.

'If you'd heard her screams, you wouldn't have been able to stand it, you'd have died yourself!'

Reşit stopped, then gently pushed open the door. The women poured in after him, and when they saw what was before them, they screamed louder than the night.

47

As I walked towards my building, I looked up at my window on the third floor. As always, one pane was open. 'That's good,' I thought, as I dragged myself up the stairs. 'In spite of everything, I must still be writing . . .'

I stopped on the second-floor landing, to catch my breath. A procession of anxious faces passed me by, and footsteps, clattering off to work. Drowsy women rushed past, and children clutching hot loaves of bread, but not a single one seemed to see me standing there, and not one so much as wished me a good morning. I was nothing in their eyes, my face no more than a distant reminder of a hundred others. And how many thousands of times had they seen someone like me, catching his breath on a second-floor landing? When I reached the third floor and pushed open my door, I still felt the same way. As I took off my shoes and padded into my study, I savoured the comfort of being a nobody.

First I opened the curtains. Then I pushed the typewriter to one side and tidied up the piles of paper. When all that was done, I picked up my glass of tea, and sat down to wait. I didn't know what I was waiting for, in fact; I kept peering down at the street but still I couldn't figure out who or what I was expecting. Or maybe I just couldn't remember.

'Would you like some tea?' my wife called through the door.

'No thanks,' I said. 'I still haven't finished this one.'

'You've left the light on,' she said, as she shut the door behind her.

I got up and turned it off.

I went back over to the window, looking down at the street as I drank my tea. The shutters had stopped clanking by now, and the simit and salep vendors had drifted off, to make way for white-capped men selling lottery tickets.

'Nothing has changed,' I said to myself. I drank what was left of my tea and was heading into the kitchen when the doorbell rang. I opened the door; it was my son. He looked surprised. 'Oh,' he said. 'You've washed all the soap off your face!' I was more surprised than he was. I stood there stunned as he came in and took off his shoes.

'Here are your Perma-Sharp razor blades,' he said, holding out the box. 'Sorry for taking so long, but the shop was closed. I had to go all the way to the other end of the street.'

'Did you get a paper?' asked my wife from the kitchen.

'Yes,' said my son. 'You'll never guess what it says.'

'What does it say?'

'A girl's been kidnapped by a bear!'

Sincan, 13.3.1990–25.9.1993

GLOSSARY

ayran: a water and yoghurt drink similar to buttermilk.

Azrael: the Angel of Death in Islam.

bismillah: Arabic for 'in the name of God'. The first word of many prayers and used as a stand-in for them.

divan saz: a seven-stringed lute-like instrument.

halay: a folk dance popular at weddings, in which the dancers link fingers or arms and dance in a line.

hamam: a Turkish bath; a large public bathhouse.

keşkek: a traditional wedding food made from beef or mutton and wheat.

Mecnun: a romantic figure from a Persian folk tale who went insane after learning that his love had been married off to another man.

menemen: a dish of scrambled eggs with tomatoes, peppers, spices and sometimes onion.

muhtar: the democratically elected headman responsible for the people of a village or neighbourhood.

rakı: an aniseed-flavoured drink similar to ouzo or arak, typically drunk with water and ice.

salep: an orchid-flavoured sweet, hot drink.

simit: a ring-shaped, crunchy type of bread.

tarhana: a soup made of wheat, yoghurt and vegetables.

watchman: a person tasked with preventing crime and keeping the civil peace in a village or neighbourhood.

yufka: a thin, unleavened bread.

Zulfiqar: the name of a legendary sword owned by the Caliph Ali.

zurna: a large wind instrument typically accompanied by a drum.

A NOTE ON THE TYPE

The text of this book is set in Fournier. Fournier is derived from the *romain du roi*, which was created towards the end of the seventeenth century from designs made by a committee of the Académie of Sciences for the exclusive use of the Imprimerie Royale. The original Fournier types were cut by the famous Paris founder Pierre Simon Fournier in about 1742. These types were some of the most influential designs of the eight and are counted among the earliest examples of the 'transitional' style of typeface. This Monotype version dates from 1924. Fournier is a light, clear face whose distinctive features are capital letters that are quite tall and bold in relation to the lower-case letters, and *decorative italics, which show the influence of the calligraphy of Fournier's time.*

ALSO AVAILABLE BY HASAN ALİ TOPTAŞ

RECKLESS

Longlisted for the FT/OppenheimerFunds Emerging Voices Award

Thirty years after completing his military service Ziya flees the spiralling turmoil of one of Turkey's great sprawling cities to seek a serene existence in a dream-like village.

Kenan – an old friend from the army – is there to greet him. However, the village does not provide the total isolation Ziya yearns for and he is forced back through the tangled web of his memory in search of his lost family and the reason why Kenan feels so extravagantly indebted to him.

Reckless masterfully blurs the boundaries between memory and reality to create a gripping tale that introduces a major writer to English-language readers.

'A wonderful and gripping story ... This is news and history made intimate. I am deeply grateful to Hasan Ali Toptaş for having told me this story and look forward to others'
NADEEM ASLAM

'Challenging, innovative, deeply humane'
TIMES LITERARY SUPPLEMENT

'A novel to be read slowly, with frequent pauses to catch your breath. Take it in small servings, to stop it interfering with your life. And beware! This book can hurt'
YENI ŞAFAK

ORDER YOUR COPY:

BY PHONE: +44 (0) 1256 302 699; **BY EMAIL:** DIRECT@MACMILLAN.CO.UK

DELIVERY IS USUALLY 3–5 WORKING DAYS. FREE POSTAGE AND PACKAGING FOR ORDERS OVER £20.

ONLINE: WWW.BLOOMSBURY.COM/BOOKSHOP

PRICES AND AVAILABILITY SUBJECT TO CHANGE WITHOUT NOTICE.

WWW.BLOOMSBURY.COM/AUTHOR/HASAN-ALI-TOPTAS

BLOOMSBURY